One Man Posse

ALSO BY MAX BRAND

One Man Posse

MAX BRAND, 1892-1944

DODD, MEAD & COMPANY

New York

One-Man Posse is comprised of "One-Man Posse," "Sleeper Pays a Debt," "Satan's Gun Rider" and "Sleeper Turns Horse Thief," which were originally published in *Mavericks Magazine* in 1934, and "Sun and Sand," which was originally published in *Western Story Magazine* in 1935.

Published by Dodd, Mead & Company, Inc.
71 Fifth Avenue, New York, N.Y. 10003
Distributed in Canada by
McClelland and Stewart Limited, Toronto
Manufactured in the United States of America
First Edition

1 2 3 4 5 6 7 8 9 10

Library of Congress Cataloging-in-Publication Data

Brand, Max, 1892-1944.
   One man posse.

   (A Silver star western)
   I. Title.   II.Series.
PS3511.A87054   1987   813'.52   86-19685
ISBN 0-396-08891-0

1

Pop Lowry blinked his faded eyes at the first shaft of the early June sun. He came to life at once, his lank, spare frame seeming to gather itself upward in layers from the tarp spread out on the grassy slope near the cluster of black rocks. His dressing was simple—merely putting on his coat and pulling on a pair of down-at-the-heel cow-side boots.

But there was something wrong with the left boot. Pop swore, pulled it off and squinted inside, his gnarled fingers exploring the insole. Then he grunted, replaced the inner sole and tugged on the footgear again. It was only then that he remembered to look about, down the slope, past where his three mules were tethered. He did not turn around in time to see a dark shadow sink into nothingness on top of the nearest black rock. Had he done so, he might have made even more haste in saddling and loading the mules.

For Pop, who lived in secret fear of being robbed of the peddler's stock which he packed by muleback over a thousand mile route, had gotten a warning at the last ranch he had visited. Wild Bill Belling was rumored to be hiding out somewhere in this territory. Wild Bill, rustler, killer and all-round bad hombre, had been the lieutenant of the notorious Charley Loder, and had made a successful getaway when a determined crowd of posse-

1

men had corralled Loder and taken him to jail. If Belling had known—as he well might, through the rustling of the leaves—that Pop Lowry had been instrumental in getting a reward placed on his head . . . the old peddler's eyes narrowed in anxiety as he passed the heel of his hand over his sweat-beaded forehead.

Abruptly he stooped and seemed to search anxiously through the short grass at his feet. Twice he straightened, twice again he searched, muttering to himself, looking more than ever like some skinny wizened creature of the wasteland who would scuttle back into hiding at the first sign of human approach.

Presently a voice, coming from behind and above him, drawled, "It's in the crack of that rock, yonder."

Pop Lowry straightened with a jerk and looked wildly about. He saw nothing at first, then made out, reclining on top of the largest black rock, a tanned youngster in his early twenties—a fellow in ragged and sun-bleached Levis, who wore a limp-brimmed colorless hat on his head and homemade moccasins on his feet.

"Sleeper!" exclaimed the startled Lowry with relief. "How long you been here?"

The question was rhetorical; Pop Lowry knew he could scarcely expect an answer, for the kid—the stray, maybe half-locoed kid called Sleeper—would talk only when he chose. Pop Lowry frowned. Then he went over to the flat rock and from the crack he lifted a long black-snake whip. He sleeked the lash through his gnarled fingers while he turned to the ragged kid.

Sleeper—"ear-notched, but mostly maverick," men said of him—had stretched himself flat on the rock with his hands under his head and let the sun beat full on his face.

"How'd you know I was lookin' for that blacksnake?" said Pop querulously.

"You couldn't be lookin' for anything else," drawled

2

the kid. "That's the only thing you didn't have. An' it had to be in that crack, 'cause the grass is too short to hide anything from eyes like yours." He yawned again.

Sleeper's blue-black hair might have been either Irish or Indian, but the deep, sea-blue of his eyes gave the former race predominance in him. As he lay there languidly stretched out, his suppleness of body suggested infinite speed of foot and hand, which had come to him from living most of his life under the roof of the sky. No one knew what happened to him in the winter; everyone—cattlemen, townspeople, miners, nesters—knew that he would appear with the first of the warm weather, when the bunch-grass and blue-joint began to get green in the bottomlands.

Sleeper said drowsily, "I wanted to talk to you about something, Pop. Talk about money."

The peddler snorted. "Money! Huh! You ain't got use for money. I always thought you lazied around, eatin' the wind you could raise. *You* don't need money."

"A thousand dollars is more than money," Sleeper said softly. "It—it's a chance, a thousand dollars is. . . ."

"What thousand?"

"The dinero you offered for the capture of that outlaw, Belling."

Lowry snorted again. "Ah-h. I didn't offer no reward for Belling. A lot of ranchers along my route, they been talking to me, saying this Belling's been raisin' hell with their herds, even killed a couple of folks, they said. I said why didn't they get together and ante up a reward for him. Then maybe fellers would be more interested in riskin' their lives tryin' to get him. That would put an end to his hellin' around."

"I got a pretty good idea how to get him. I aim to get that thousand dollars, Pop."

"You do, eh?" the peddler smiled expansively. He could well afford to take a little time to fool with Sleeper.

3

Besides—maybe the kid might have some ideas. Sleeper got around in all sorts of strange places where a hunted man might hole up. "Well, then, if you're so smart, just how'd you go about trackin' him?"

Sleeper's blue eyes blinked as he scratched his head. "Why, they say his horse was caught a few days ago down near Plummett. This Belling's a powerful big man and that horse was maybe the best friend he had. He can't ride just any horse that happens to come along. I'd turn his horse loose and track it. Maybe it would lead to some of Belling's hide-outs. A feller could do it easy, if he knew that horse, marked the shape of its hoof-prints and the length of its walking step and its trot and its canter and its gallop. Belling'd be asleep, and then—"

"Hell!" crowed the peddler. "Belling'd wake up an' jump right on that horse. By the time any man had a chance to take a shot at him, Belling'd be long gone. I never heard any such crazy notion! You think a horse is a bloodhound?"

"That's what I do," said Sleeper, and he relaxed more completely than ever in the sun.

Lowry moved to get into the saddle. "Yah! You mean you'd of daydreamed till it would have seemed like you'd done it—but you wouldn't dare to come within ten miles of a killer like Belling!" He put one foot into the stirrup.

"It *was* sort of scary," agreed Sleeper. "But I got him. That's why I wanted to see you about the thousand dollars."

"You got him where?" shouted Lowry.

"Over there in a buggy," said Sleeper. He sat up and pointed. "Right there on the trail."

Lowry leaped around the corner of the rock and saw a ramshackle old buggy, each of whose wheels leaned in a different direction. A big man was lashed into the seat beside the driver's place, a big man without a hat

4

and with flaming red hair that stood up on end as though in a wind. Lowry noted that he was so securely tied he had given up struggling with the raw-hide thongs that bound him.

"Belling!" yelled Lowry, and started on a run towards the buggy.

"Get up, Pokey!" called Sleeper.

The mule which was harnessed between the shafts at once struck out on a brisk trot.

"Hey! Whoa! Whoa, mule! Whoa, you fool!" shouted Lowry.

"Pokey won't stop for anybody but me," said Sleeper.

"Damn it!" cried Lowry. "Stop the fool mule before it runs over the edge of the cliff!"

"Whoa, boy," called Sleeper, and the mule stopped. "So what about the thousand dollars?" yawned Sleeper.

"Thousand dollars? You don't expect me to carry that much around with me, do you?" asked Lowry in a complaining voice.

"Just give me your left boot, and that will do," answered Sleeper.

Pop Lowry started so violently that his feet almost left the ground. He looked down at his left boot.

"I'd as soon have what's under the insole of that boot as any thousand dollars," said Sleeper.

"Kid," growled the peddler, "you know too doggone much."

"Money makes a feller want to scratch," said Sleeper. "And your foot itched when you shoved it into that boot a while ago."

Lowry stared for a moment. Then he pulled off his boot, took the insole out of it, and produced several rumpled greenbacks. He drew on the boot again and advanced towards Sleeper.

Sleeper pulled out a heavy bone-handled hunting knife and began to spin it high in the air. When it came down, he caught it on the top of the thumb-nail, making it land on the point and stand straight up.

"Great thunder!" gasped Lowry. "Where'd you learn that trick?"

"Easy," said Sleeper. "It just takes time to learn, and I've got plenty of time. You jerk your hand down as the point of the knife hits the nail, and the point hardly makes a scratch."

"Suppose you don't move your hand fast enough, your thumb is split through the end?"

"Yeah. But you want to move your hand fast enough."

The peddler held out the money in his left hand. With the left hand, Sleeper accepted it; in his right hand he held the long knife, so sharp that the light seemed to be dripping off the point.

Lowry looked at that sleepily smiling, tanned face, and then glanced at the knife. "You're a thousand dollars richer than I ever expected to see you, kid. But you done a mighty good job," said Lowry.

"It just took a little time. Thanks," said Sleeper. He stood up on the edge of the rock and jumped. It was ten feet to the ground below, but he landed on legs which flexed as such perfect springs that the brim of his tattered hat hardly flopped with the shock. He stepped to the buggy and, pulling on the knot-end of the lariat which bound Belling, he set the big man free.

Belling, shaking the bonds from his body, leaped out of the buggy with a roar. But the rope had gripped his big muscles until they were numb. He staggered and almost fell.

Then Lowry's calm voice said: "Steady, Belling. I wanta talk to you a bit before I take you to jail." An enormous, old-fashioned hogleg was in his fist.

The red-headed outlaw turned towards the peddler with a scowl. "You bought me, did you? I'm gonna see you in hell for this!" he declared.

Sleeper was already in the driver's place; Pokey broke into a trot.

"Hey, wait. Hey, Sleeper!" shouted the peddler.

But Sleeper rattled down the trail in the old buggy without seeming to hear the shouts.

2

Sleeper leaned against the fence that surrounded the big corral. Inside, a golden chestnut stallion was being led back and forth. The kid had in one hand a piece of soft white pine; with the other hand he used a knife, drawing from the pine stick shavings so thin that the sun shone through them as easily as through ice.

He was so absorbed that he appeared to be paying little attention to the words of the men around him, though the entire town of White Water had turned out to attend the sale of Careless. There was reason for the excitement. In the first place, the big stallion, Careless, was the finest horse that White Water had ever seen. In the second place, it was known that this horse had been the favorite mount of Charlie Loder, that vaunted bandit who was now serving a twenty-five year term in prison, so far as anyone knew. In the third place, it was equally well known that the possession of the horse had descended to that brutal former partner of Loder—Wild Bill Belling. And fourthly, and perhaps it was this that had brought interest to a fever pitch, Careless had been stolen out of the corral of Sheriff Bill Collins, had been absent for five days, and then had been returned, in perfect condition, and in the middle of the night, to that same corral.

Sleeper, who could have told something about the stealing and the return of the stallion, raised his head as he heard a man near him say: "Whoever buys Careless ain't gonna have him long. Not with Charlie Loder on the trail again."

That made Sleeper say: "Is Charlie Loder on the trail again?"

The tall cowboy who had just spoken turned and glanced with a familiar contempt at Sleeper.

"Don't you know nothing, Sleeper?" he asked. "Ain't you heard that Loder busted loose out of prison last week?"

"He don't hear nothin', and if he did, he couldn't savvy it," laughed the companion of the tall cowpuncher.

Sleeper paid no heed. As for the opinion of his fellows, they never troubled him a great deal. How to get the next meal with the least outlay of effort was his daily problem. What other men said and felt mattered less than nothing to him.

Here he heard Sheriff Bill Collins saying loudly: "There's room up there in front for you, Mister Williams. Yes, sir; there's room up in front for you no matter what's happenin' in White Water."

Sleeper drew the thinnest of the shavings from the face of the glistening bit of pine. He saw the rich rancher, Henry Williams, ride through the crowd with the sheriff beside him. And at the shoulder of the rancher appeared his daughter, Kate, the beauty of White Water.

Here a sudden burst of neighing made Sleeper turn. He saw Careless pull back on the lead rope and heard him trumpet a call for freedom.

Sleeper whistled, a thin, sharp note, not overloud, and the golden stallion at once stopped his neigh, stopped

8

his resistance. He turned his lordly head towards the kid who said: "Steady, boy!"

Careless nickered a soft note of recognition and submitted to the handling of the man who was leading him.

"Where'd *you* git to know Careless?" demanded the tall cowpuncher.

"We've had some talks together," answered Sleeper quietly.

"He can talk horse talk better than man-talk, maybe?" suggested the cowboy's companion.

"He maybe can talk horse talk," said the tall cowboy, "but he ain't got horse-sense."

There was a loud laugh, at this, but Sleeper was again deep in the problems of his whittling. He seemed to pay no heed. Not a trace of color appeared in his face, nor did he appear as if he had heard the affront.

A moment later, he had his shoulder flicked by the end of a quirt.

It was the sheriff, bawling out: "Sleeper, what you doing there in a front seat? Get out and let your superiors have a show, will you? Here's Mr. Williams and his daughter need a place close to the fence. Move back and let them step in!"

"No, Sheriff!" protested the clear, quick voice of the girl. "We don't want to displace anyone."

"You ain't displacing anybody when you displace Sleeper," said the sheriff. "He ain't even got a name! So how could you be displacing anything?"

Sleeper did not protest. He retreated smoothly through the crowd and allowed rich Mr. Williams to take that coveted place near the fence, with his daughter before him. She turned her brown eyes anxiously towards Sleeper, and her lips said silently: "Sorry!" Her eyes said: "Sorry!" also. But Sleeper paid no heed.

He drifted back through the crowd after the sheriff's horse, and as big Bill Collins reached the outskirts of

9

the crowd, Sleeper rapped his knuckles on the taps of the McClellan stirrups.

"Yeah—yeah?" snapped Collins, looking down. Then he softened. "Oh, it's you, is it? Well, kid, I just wanted your place at the fence for Mister Williams. I didn't want to drag you out of the crowd."

Sleeper, with an odd, fixed smile, looked up at the sheriff. "You remembered me today, Sheriff," he said. "I'll be remembering you tomorrow."

"Hey? What do you mean, you fool?" demanded the sheriff with a frown.

Sleeper's smile persisted. It was open-eyed, steady; and it made cold chills crawl, for no reason in particular, up the sheriff's spine. He was angered and a little ashamed because he felt this reaction, and he didn't know why.

"I wanta tell you something, kid," said he. "I got a mind to run you out of this town, anyway. We don't want vagrants around here, we don't want know-nothin's nor do-nothin's."

But Sleeper was already drifting away.

He heard a voice call: "Here's where you get your genu-wine silver saddle fittings, gents. Mexican silver conchos, inlaid bits and buckles. Here's where you get 'em, at the cheapest price. Anybody want any more?"

It was the peddler, Pop Lowry, his nasal voice ringing through the noise of the crowd. His appearance was a little unusual, for his hat was worn crookedly to accommodate a thick white bandage that was wound about his head.

Sleeper paused and stared at him.

"Why, hello, Sleeper," said the peddler. "I been wanting to see you." He tossed his trinkets into the mule's alforjas and stepped closer to Sleeper.

"Hello, Pop," said Sleeper. "Did Belling get away?"

"You'd think I'd leave him get away?" growled Lowry.

"How would I know? You weren't paying a thousand

dollars just to put him in jail, were you?" Sleeper's voice was ironic.

Lowry blinked. "You're loco—always been loco, Sleeper," And then, in a lower voice: "How many people you told about catching Belling, kid?"

"Why should I tell anybody?" asked Sleeper.

"Why? Why should you tell—after the way you captured Belling? Son, everybody in town must of heard you crow by the time I got down here."

"Was that why you put on the bandage, Pop?" asked Sleeper without a smile.

"I dunno what you're talking about," the peddler growled.

"Just to show how hard you fought to keep him when he took you by surprise. Didn't he take you by surprise?"

"He sure did!" agreed Pop Lowry fervently. And then he added in a softer growl: "You—you mean you haven't told a soul about catching—him?"

"No. You damn fool, would that double my income?"

"Sleeper, stop whittling and listen here. You got parts, somehow. You got quality, maybe. The rest of these boggle-heads, they can't see it. But for years I been waiting for you to grow up; and that time has come."

"You want me to catch Belling again?"

"I want—listen to me—somebody's going to bid plenty dinero to get this horse, Careless."

"Maybe you're right," conceded Sleeper, "whoever gets him—*if* he gets him," he added grimly.

"Whoever gets that horse is going to lead him away. And the man that leads Careless away is going to meet Belling and turn the horse over to him. I know—never mind how I know. And then Belling is going to ride on until he meets another man, and then the two of them are going to ride to Chimney Creek."

"Then you could get some head-money at Chimney Creek, if you wait for the pair of them there, and if you

11

had the—guts, eh?" suggested Sleeper. "There's a price on Belling now, even without *your* thousand."

"Wait a minute, son, I'm going to trust you. The thing is this—maybe Belling *won't* ride with the other man to Chimney Creek. Understand? And wherever Belling goes, I want you to follow him; and when you've got where he hides out with the other man, I want you to ride back and tell me. I'm going to be in the old shack east of White Water. You know, where Ike Matthews used to live."

"I know. And I bring you back to the two of them, I suppose?"

"Yeah. You got it. You bring me back to the two of them." The peddler's eyes turned into bright slits.

"What's the price?"

"I'll give you five days' wages—ten dollars. No, by God, I'll make it twenty!"

Sleeper smiled. "I've got a new price. I've turned bounty hunter," he said. "Just exactly one thousand dollars."

"Oh, God!" intoned the peddler. "You think I'm made of money? You gone loco?"

"Maybe you had another bill in your boots," suggested Sleeper. "Or if you didn't, find somebody else who can trail Careless."

The peddler pulled off his hat and wiped his bald head with the flat of his hand. "Well," he said, "I dunno. I'll pay you a thousand dollars spot cash for the job—and damn you, Sleeper, for askin' that much."

"I risk my head and you risk a few pennies," said Sleeper, cheerfully, "but maybe your man *won't* lead Careless away."

"I'm telling you what'll happen. Don't ask fool questions," answered Pop Lowry.

Sleeper's eyes narrowed the least bit. "Tell me another thing. Before Charlie Loder went to jail—"

The peddler started violently. He took a step closer

to Sleeper. "Who put Loder's name into this game?" he demanded.

"I did," said Sleeper. "I'm asking you—before Charlie Loder went to prison, wasn't he running around with Kate Williams?"

"Huh?" gasped the peddler. "What the hell difference does that make?"

Sleeper said nothing. He just grinned.

"Well," explained the peddler, "he was running around with her, yeah, you could call it that. Why not? Best-looking man and the best-looking girl? Why shouldn't they go together?"

"Of course they should," agreed Sleeper.

"Well—keep your mouth shut; maybe I'll be useful to you," Pop Lowry said.

And, at that moment, the voice of the auctioneer began to bawl: "Ready, gents; loosen up your pants pockets; trot out your hard cash. We're sellin' the finest horse that ever went under the hammer, boys! From barrel to hocks, he's a real man's horse—he's had to be, 'cause he's been grain-fed without a bit of hay. The owners of this horse have had to travel far and fast and never bothered about a bill of sale. Look at him, gents—see that sleek arch; the shape of that head; you can't afford to miss this one chance! Gents"—and with a look toward Kate Williams—"ladies, I'm askin' for an opening bid— on Careless!"

"Two hundred and fifty dollars," came an excited yell. And with that offer there was a loud burst of derisive laughter.

3

The bid seemed foolish enough, considering the quality of the stallion which was still pacing up and down the corral. Now he threw up his head and neighed again. He was like leaf gold—and he burned in the sunlight.

But still, two hundred and fifty dollars was a good deal of money for a horse in a community which knew that a good cow-pony could be bought for fifty. For a hundred and fifty dollars, one could get a trained cutting horse which would follow a calf through a herd of cows and turning short, would work almost faster than the thought of the ordinary rider.

Two hundred and fifty dollars was a good deal—and yet, there stood that great golden stallion!

As the neighing died out, a man called to the auctioneer: "He's laughin' at you, Jerry!"

"Two hundred and fifty dollars," shouted the auctioneer, "offered by Mr. Jeremiah Bangor—thank you, Jerry; thank you for starting the dance but I reckon that nobody ain't gonna walk off with Careless for a price like that. Careless is his name—careless have been the gents that have rode him."

"Three hundred!" said the voice. And then it went up to five hundred. It was a lot of money when you could hire a good cowhand for forty a month and beans. Five hundred for a bit of horseflesh enclosed within a single skin!

There was a pause. Then, suddenly a voice said: "And ten!"

"Shorty Joe Bennett!" murmured someone. "Shorty Joe must be diggin' down to the toe of the sock. Is he drunk?"

Shorty Joe Bennett stood on the lowest bar of the corral fence. He blinked as all eyes turned upon him and his face turned a deep red. But he kept his grip on the top rail of the fence with those tense, white-knuckled hands, and with his eyes he kept his hold on the burning beauty of the stallion.

"Five hundred and ten dollars bid by Shorty Joe Bennett!" shouted the auctioneer. "Good work, Joe! Come on, boys! Everybody's in this. Careless is worth any man's entire spread. Five hundred is plenty, but he's worth more than that. There's a horse that nobody will catch you on!"

A girl's voice cried: "Fifty!"

"Five hundred and fifty offered by Miss Kate Williams!" called the auctioneer. There was applause. The girl's blue eyes were shining. What a picture she would make on the back of that stallion!

The sheriff himself roared out: "Six hundred!" His face was swollen. He pulled at his soft, tieless collar to give himself better breathing.

"*And* ten!" droned the voice of Shorty Joe Bennett.

The sheriff flung both arms into the air.

"By God, I offered all I could!" he cried. Tears were in his eyes.

"Six-fifty!" called Kate Williams pleasantly, after turning to look at her father. There was a shout of enthusiasm.

"Sixty!" snapped Joe Bennett. He was an ugly man with a vast jaw and a face that sloped steadily back to the roots of his hair. He looked like an ugly overgrowth of a dwarf.

There was a silence. Kate Williams turned to her father. There was a brief colloquy between them, the rancher shaking his head.

"Six hundred and sixty dollars offered for this glorious stallion!" cried the auctioneer. "Do I hear an up?"

"Seven hundred!" cried the voice of Kate Williams.

At this, a cheer was raised.

"*And* ten," said the dour Joe Bennett. Silence followed. It was a gross insult to even think of such a fellow as Bennett on the back of the great chestnut.

And then another voice said, so quietly that it was hardly heard: "Eight hundred dollars!"

All heads snapped around. "Sleeper, d'you mean that you're biddin' or are you jokin'?" asked the auctioneer.

There was a roar of laughter. The town lazy man, the nameless tramp, the idler Sleeper, bidding eight hundred dollars?

For answer, Sleeper held up a stiff sheaf of greenbacks in his left hand. And the laughter was wiped from every face. A little lane opened before Sleeper, and he advanced from the rear of the crowd to the fence.

"And ten!" snarled Joe Bennett.

It was getting to be a lot of money.

People could see Kate Williams pleading with her father, but this time his shake of the head was obdurate and final.

"Nine hundred!" cried Sleeper loudly.

And now a sudden yell went up from the throats of the audience. They had become, all of them, mere spectators. There remained two fanatics who loved a horse more than they loved money. One of them was the deformed Joe Bennett. The other was the town tramp, in rags. People gripped each other by the arm, and stared, and waited with hungry ears.

"Mister Sleeper!" yelled the auctioneer, giving the name a title because of the new respect which suddenly was filling his breast. "Did I hear you say nine hundred dollars?"

Sleeper, from his pocket, added another bill to the sheaf in his left, raised hand.

"Yes," he said. "Nine hundred dollars!"

And now a very strange thing happened, for the great

16

stallion, hearing this voice, whirled suddenly, snatched the leadrope out of the hand of the man controlling him, and rushed for the fence, at the spot where Sleeper stood.

There, people shrank back, thinking that the great monster would leap the bars. Instead, he skidded to a halt, and then thrust his head between the bars and into the arms of Sleeper.

What a shout answered that demonstration from the fierce horse! Men beat one another about the shoulders. Women screamed.

"And ten!" groaned the voice of Shorty Joe Bennett.

"Nine hundred and ten offered!" said the auctioneer. He stood half-crouched, sweating, excited like a runner about to start for a race. "Do I hear an up?"

"Dad!" pleaded the voice of Kate Williams. "*Do* help Sleeper!"

"An infernal low tramp? A worthless idler? Help him?" exploded the rancher. "I'll see him damned first!"

And everyone heard that.

Sleeper, standing close by with one hand stroking the head of Careless, turned a little and took off his tattered hat and bowed to the girl. "I have to have him with my own money—not with gifts," he said. And turning back toward the auctioneer, he cried loudly: "One thousand dollars!"

Pandemonium followed. Men were climbing the rails to see better. They saw, among other things, that Sleeper had added another bill to the sheaf which he held in his left hand.

The cheering, the wild yelling lasted for some time, but as it died down, the inevitable voice of Shorty Joe Bennett growled: "*And* ten!"

The auctioneer cried through the deadly silence: "A thousand and ten dollars offered for Careless. People that understand would offer two thousand, three thou-

17

sand! Gentlemen, remember yourselves!" He looked at rich rancher Williams, as he said this.

The girl, people saw, was staring toward Sleeper, the tramp. And then they saw that Sleeper's head had fallen in utter defeat.

"Going for a thousand and ten dollars!" cried the auctioneer. "Going to Shorty Joe Bennett for a thousand and ten dollars—do I hear an up?"

And that same tall cowpuncher who had mocked at Sleeper before exclaimed: "I got forty dollars, Sleeper, and it's yours. Give him an up, kid!"

"I won't buy him with borrowed money," said Sleeper. He lifted his head and nodded: "Thanks, old timer!"

People were more stunned by this, perhaps, than by all the strange performance which had gone before.

"Going!" yelled the auctioneer, waving both arms. "Going for a thousand and ten; going—going—think of it, gentlemen, the finest horse that ever stepped in White Water—for a thousand and ten—going—going —gone to Joe Bennett! Sold, Joe! Shorty, Careless belongs to you."

But Careless was paying no attention to this. He was trying, with his prehensile upper lip, to get into the coat pocket of Sleeper, and Sleeper, with deeply bowed head, was stroking him vaguely across the forehead.

Shorty Joe marched across the ring and grabbed the lead-rope of Careless and drew him away.

Sleeper, gripping the rail of the fence, made no move until he heard the voice of the girl say: "I'm sorry, Sleeper! I'm terribly sorry! You loved him. I can see that!"

He lifted his eyes and saw her through a haze which told him that he was looking through tears. But what amazed him was to see that tears were openly in her own eyes.

"Here, Kate, here!" said her father, taking her by the arm. "All damned nonsense! If he has a thousand, where did he get it?"

"By risking my neck to get it!" answered Sleeper. There were other men who heard him say this, and they were willing to re-tell it in the barroom afterwards. "Did you ever get a penny of your money the same way, Mister Williams?"

But Williams made no answer. He hurriedly took his daughter through the crowd.

4

Sleeper could have remained in White Water and drunk away days and days at the expense of other men, because by this effort he had become, suddenly, a sort of minor hero. In a country where all men loved horses, he, the tramp, had proved that he loved a horse better than the rest. In a subtle way, he had shamed the great Henry C. Williams by offering up his skin, whereas Williams would not give even the price of a few of his thousands of fat steers.

Two people emerged from this with credit—Kate Williams and Sleeper. And Shorty Joe Bennett emerged with the stallion, but with the suspicion of the crowd attached to him. For Shorty, all his life, had never done anything better than cheat at cards.

Sleeper, working his way through the crowd, avoided the hearty invitations which poured in on him. He found the peddler walking at his side, saying: "What's the matter, kid? Would you give every penny to get a horse? Better have some place to go before you buy the way of getting there."

19

And Sleeper, looking him in the eye, answered: "You're a crook, Pop. I've always known that you were a crook. Today, I'm sure of it. But I'm damned if I care how much of a crook you are so long as I can get Careless!"

He expected a curse in response. He was amazed to hear the peddler say: "Well, well, well! It's always with a fellow like you that I do the biggest business, Sleeper. I thought you was worth your price before. But now I'll pay you two thousand, if you bring me to Belling and his partner—any place but in Chimney Creek canyon!"

Sleeper seemed not to hear him, and walked hastily away.

Through the late afternoon, through the twilight, Shorty Joe Bennett led the stallion by devious paths and buried trails across the hills. Many a time he stopped and looked back, and each time he did so, a form sank to the ground behind a rock or glided behind a tree to shelter.

And then, in a deep, dark hollow, Sleeper saw his man greeted by a rider who paused only a moment, took the reins of the stallion, and went on.

After that, it was hard work—very hard. To follow a trotting horse on foot requires the best muscle and the best wind of a well-trained athlete. But Sleeper was well-trained. Those endless wanderings of his through the hills had given him a body of tough fibers. He was a creature of whalebone and fire. And now he added to his strength all the power of his soul. For he was on the trail of the one thing in the world that he wanted—the golden stallion, Careless!

Darkness came. Part of the time he ran by his knowledge of the land, sighting towards this gap in the hills or that forested ravine. But again, where there were several courses to choose from, he would crawl on hands and knees, lighting matches, until he found again the print of hoofs which were as well known to him as human faces to ordinary eyes.

That was how he covered the difficult corners of his assignment. He was thinking little of the two thousand dollars which had been promised to him by the strange peddler. He was thinking of Careless only and how the great stallion had come to his voice.

With a groaning eagerness, he stuck to the trail, still running when his lungs were on fire, when his knees failed him, when his head was pulled over on one shoulder by the immensity of his exertion.

And often, as he passed some running water, he wanted to throw himself headlong into the little stream and cool the heat of his blood. But he dared not waste even an instant.

Otherwise, perhaps, he would have missed the spectacle, by starlight, of two riders, not one, lifting against the horizon.

Two—not one. And the words of the peddler had come true. Big red-headed Belling had led the golden stallion and had given him to a companion.

Who could that man be? Who had placed the money for the purchase in the hands of Shorty Bennett? Who was there whom Belling feared or loved enough, in all this world, to force him to give up Careless?

What was the interest and what was the information of the peddler?

Where were these two riders bound?

Certainly, they were not headed for Chimney Creek. To what point, then? And how was he to get back to the old shack east of White Water in order to warn Pop?

No, he was first to run the pair to ground. He, with his unaided legs, and the pair of them on fine horses!

Why was it that Pop Lowry wanted them to go to Chimney Creek?

These questions he repeated to himself over and over again in a sort of hypnotic dream, his brain going weary with the words. And then he heard the thunders of the cataracts of White Water Creek and dipped into the

21

great, dark ravine through which the creek ploughed its way.

He ran as fast as he could, but his knees were gone. There was no spring in his ankles. He had to swing his leaden, nerveless legs from the hips, and use his will power to make every stride. And then he saw, like an eye opening through the darkness, a single ray of light. He stopped. The light had disappeared as though it had been one ray shot from a dark lantern. He pushed through a hedge of tall brush close beside the rushing of White Water Creek and saw the ray of light again. Going ahead carefully, he made out at last the lines of a cabin almost over-clouded by a great growth of trees. Still closer, he came on the dim silhouettes of two horses, and even the blanket of the night could not altogether hide the gleam of the silken coat of Careless.

A faint whicker of recognition came from the big horse. Sleeper stood close, his arm around the neck of the stallion, and listened to a muttering of voices inside the cabin. But he could not make out the words because the roar of the cataracts, which were only a little way down the creek, filled the air with a burden of sound.

He stood back from the cabin, and the stallion tried to follow but was pushed away. At those pushing hands, Careless sniffed curiously and nipped very gently Sleeper's sleeve.

But Sleeper was watching a spot of dull light which broke through the roof and painted a round of faint silver on the foliage of a tree overhead. A moment later, like a cat, he was climbing the log wall, then stretching himself up the slant of the roof. It was the flimsiest sort of an affair of thatch and cross-branches. It had not been patched for years, and it gave with a slight sagging and shuddering under Sleeper's weight. But he continued until he was able to look down through the hole in the thatch at what was happening below. There he saw

22

Belling digging vigorously with a rusty spade by lantern light. He was opening up a hole in the earthen floor of the shack.

By Belling's side a tall fellow walked up and down, a man with a handsome face full of command. He was not more than thirty. He had the clean cut quality of a youth and the strength of maturity about him. And his face was that of Charlie Loder. Sleeper remained at his post with a slight chill running through his blood. He would have felt the same emotion if he had come on a sleek-sided panther, facing him in a lonely, narrow mountain trail.

"Belling," said Loder, "how many times have your hands itched to come up here and dig the stuff out?"

"Fifty times," said Belling, chuckling. "But every time I got the itch, I remembered that no jail would hold you long, Charlie. So I just swallered and held hard."

"This peddler—old Pop Lowry," said Loder. "You say that he knows there's loot somewhere in the hills?"

"He's got his trap set over in Chimney Creek," answered Belling, laughing again. "He had me in a hole and I had to talk up. I said all I knew was that the stuff was in Chimney Creek but that you were the only one that knew the exact spot. So I suppose he's got half a dozen thugs over there waiting for us. Him and me are to split two ways."

"Belling," said Loder, "either you're pretty square, or you're damned afraid of me."

"Wasn't I right?" demanded Belling. "*Did* the jail hold you?"

Loder laughed.

"But salting down that guard—that won't do you any good with the Williams girl," said Belling, driving the old shovel deep into the ground.

"She's so crazy about me," said Loder, "that it won't make any difference. Desperate man, struggling for his rights of freedom—you know. She'll be sorrier than ever for me."

"You mean she thinks you got clean hands all the way through?"

"That's what I mean," chuckled Loder. "There's no fool like a female fool."

"But how you gonna work the marriage gag when you're already married?"

"Leave that to me, feller. I'll show her a gent who looks like a minister, and I'll put a real gold ring on her finger. And after that—her old man can buy her way out. That's all I ever had my eye on—his coin. And he's got plenty of it."

"She's a pretty kid," said Belling.

"Yeah? She doesn't interest me," declared Loder. "Too damn sweet and clean. The trouble with a girl like that, she's got no background. She don't mean anything. She don't understand."

"No?" queried Belling.

"No. She don't understand. She won't smoke; she won't sit down and have a drink with you. How you going to spend time with a girl like that? And I've always got to be watching my tongue when I'm with her. One crack and I'd be ruined."

"She's sure loco about you."

"Because she thinks that poor Charlie Loder has had so much bad luck. That's the reason. The world has used poor Charlie so badly that she's going to make everything up to him. She believes in me the way an Irishman believes in any lost cause."

Here the shovel of Belling grated on metal; and Loder suddenly leaned over the hole in the ground. The top of a large tin was now exposed, and Belling drew a five gallon oil can out of the earth.

"Here it is, chief!" he exclaimed.

"Open it up!" snapped Loder.

It was accordingly opened by Belling, who first took out a flat package wrapped in oiled silk.

"You remember? That's you and Myrtle."

"That's right," said Loder. "I was all sure stampeded by Myrtle in those days. Damn her! I wouldn't be caught with her picture on me and that's why we buried it with the coin."

"She still crazy about you?" asked Belling.

"No girl is crazy about a man after she marries him," said Loder bitterly. "She's been running around with a dance hall dude for the last six months and she won't get a divorce because she still thinks that she can mine some dough out of me. She's out for the money, is Myrtle. Let me have a look."

He opened the package and drew out a photograph of a woman in a bridal veil. Dimly from his spying place, Sleeper could make out the sweep of the white garment.

"There was a girl, anyway," said Loder. "Crooked—sure. The morals of a field mouse. But you could have a good time with her. She'd stake her last peso on the cards. Drink anything with a kick in it. Smoke anything that burned. I'm sort of sorry about Myrtle. And I had to bury her face along with the cash, did I? Listen, Belling—a year ago I was a lot younger. I was sort of a sentimental fool then."

"You sort of liked her," answered Belling. "My God, I hope none of this stuff has gone and molded on us!"

"It'd be bad luck for you if any of it was gone!" said the voice of Loder, suddenly turned to iron.

Belling, stopping in his work of unwrapping the treasure, looked suddenly up at his chief. "Yeah, you'd kill me, I guess," he said thoughtfully.

"Come out of it!" commanded Loder. "I know you're straight. You're the only man in the world that I'd trust, Belling."

It was finished after several wrappings of tarpaulin

25

had been untied. And under the eye of Sleeper lay several neat stacks of greenbacks. Pressure and earth-damp had compacted them a little and rounded the stacks at the corners.

"You wouldn't think that a hundred and ten thousand would look so small, would you?" asked Loder.

"Yeah, you wouldn't think it," said Belling. "We split it fifty-fifty?"

"Fifty-fifty?" shouted Loder.

"Hey—wait—" exclaimed Belling. "Any way you want is the way we'll split it. I thought you used to say it was an even cut?"

"Sure—fifty-fifty's all right," said Loder, slowly.

"No. You're sour on the idea. Make it anything you want. Sixty for you and forty for me; seventy for you and thirty for me. Break it any way you please. You mean more than the cash to me, Charlie."

"Fifty-fifty," said Loder, calmly. But there was a curiously reflective light in his eye.

Belling exclaimed: "What the devil's that?"

He had reason to look up, and so had Loder, for the whole section of the roof on which Sleeper lay had cracked and sagged, the rotten old branches yielding under the steady pressure. Vainly, Sleeper tried to slip away, down the slope of the roof; at his first movement, there was a loud crackling and rending. The whole support disappeared and he dropped in a confusion of rotten thatch and breaking branches onto the floor of the cabin, with the yell of the two surprised men ringing in his ears.

He rebounded from the floor as swiftly as any cat and leaped for the door. He would have made it and the safety of the thick night outside if his foot had not caught in one of the crooked boughs. He fell flat on his back and looked up into the leveled gun in the hand of Loder.

"It's Sleeper—it's the kid!" exclaimed Loder.

"It's the coyote that caught me and turned me over to Pop Lowry!" shouted Belling. "He's trailed me again.

By God, he's got second sight or he couldn't of follered through a night like this!"

"If he's got second sight," said Loder, "maybe he can see the corner of hell that he's goin to. Fan him, Belling."

Struggling was a folly. Sleeper did not struggle. He allowed his only weapon to be taken. It was that same long hunting knife which was almost a part of his mind, he was so expert in the use of it.

"Stand up!" snapped Loder.

Sleeper rose. Belling blocked the way to the door. He picked a length of twine from his pocket. "Slippery as a damned snake!" he commented. "When he caught me, it was like a wild cat had dropped on top of me. I couldn't do nothing."

"You mean that skinny kid handled you?" asked Loder contemptuously.

"Wait a minute," said Belling.

He tied the unresisting hands of Sleeper behind his back. Then, with a single jerk, he ripped a sleeve away.

"Look at there!" he said. "Look at the twisting of them muscles over the shoulder. Look at that forearm. The harder you sock at him, the worse you get hurt. After he got my gun, I tried to mob him. I nearly busted myself in two, trying to murder him. He had me flat in a minute. And he wasn't even breathing."

"I'd like to try him," said Loder.

"Don't you do it!" cautioned Belling. "Not even when his hands is tied, because his feet is hands, too. That's one thing that I found out."

"Kid," said Loder, "I'd like to try you, but I've got an appointment with a girl, and I'm late for it already. How long were you up there on the roof?"

"Just got there when the thing caved in," said Sleeper calmly.

"You're cool," said Loder. "You'll need to be icy, though, where you're going."

"Have we gotta plant off?" asked Belling.

"What you think, you fool?" demanded Loder.

"I don't think," said Belling. "He seems kind of young, is all."

"If he followed us tonight, he's a cat and can see in the dark. I don't want any cats on my trail, brother. We'll give him a chance to save one of his nine lives. We'll chuck him in the creek with his hands tied and see what he can do."

"With his hands tied?" exclaimed Belling. "Why, there ain't anybody hardly, that could get out of that current even with both hands free."

"It's the only chance we'll give him," said Loder. "If you can call it a chance. Grab him and start him moving, Belling!"

He added: "Wait a minute." And, taking the photograph of himself and his wife in its wrapping, he thrust it inside the breast of Sleeper's shirt. "Take this to hell with you, kid." he said. "Myrtle will be down there before long, if I have my way; and you can show her what I sent ahead of her. Give her my love, will you?"

He laughed, then he marched with Belling and Sleeper out into the night.

On the verge of the creek, where a high rock made the bank, they paused. The spray of the whipping currents rose as high as Sleeper's face. Down the stream he could see a streak of white which marked the commencement of the first cataract. The world was slipping away from him with the sweep of the stream.

"Shall we heave him in?" asked Belling.

"Wait a minute," answered Loder. "You show him the way!"

His gun spat red and Belling dropped to the rock, rolled over the edge of it, and spilled into the stream. Sleeper saw the sudden jerk as the current caught the body and snatched it whirling away.

"There's your fifty-fifty split!" said Loder calmly.

28

5

Murder seemed a small thing with that uproar of the creek in the ears and the speed of the current making a wind.

"Now, you!" said Loder, and swung the weight of his gun at the head of Sleeper. But Sleeper was already over the edge of the rock, springing out as far as he could. For his one chance in a million to live was to get himself across the creek to the farther shore. He struck the water hard, went under with his breath held, and then came to the surface, spinning out of the stream. He could swim well enough in calm water by kicking out with his legs only, but he saw that now that way was totally futile. He used that moment when he was above water to send a long, shrilling whistle through the air. He had called Careless with it many a time before; and though he knew it was vain to ask the great horse to venture into this maelstrom, he sent out the call and his last hope with it.

Then he was under water again. The stream shot him forward like a log. He had to snatch at breath in split seconds of opportunity. And he saw above him a wheeling, swaying world with the thunder of the cataracts running closer to him every moment. The stone teeth of the falls would be tearing him before long.

Then he saw, running along the bank with gigantic strides and seeming to be racing through the sky, the great form of Careless. The neighing of the big horse pierced the thundering of the creek.

Careless disappeared.

However great his affection for Sleeper, the stallion

must have shrunk away when he saw the leaping of the spray above White Water Creek. And Sleeper hardened his mind for the last moment of existence.

Something like a shadow fell across his mind's eye. With a new swirl of the current, he saw that it was the undaunted horse which, half lost in the smother of the stream, gained footing in the shallows of the creek and losing hoof-hold again in a moment, still struggled forward.

He was close. He was there beside Sleeper, and moving past him. A swinging stirrup clouted Sleeper's head. He snapped at it with his teeth and caught a hold which he kept with a frantic effort. And Careless, neighing as though in triumph, floundered on towards the farther shore.

There was little chance for Sleeper to breathe. Most of the time his head was under water as the currents streamed him out from the stirrup leather that sustained him. And behind him he heard the cataracts shouting louder as the water beat the stallion down stream.

When he had a chance to draw fresh breath and look up, he could see that the ears of the stallion were desperately flattened. He looked like some terrible snake-headed monster out of a primeval swamp.

But there was still hope, as the farther shore drew nearer, until it seemed to Sleeper that White Water Creek gathered all its forces, lurching upwards, and then whirling with a great smother of foam and spray. The stallion was picked up like so much dead wood and spun around and down the wash of the stream.

The roar of the cataracts seemed to be shouting from the skies. And then came a halt that almost jerked the teeth from the head of Sleeper. His body streamed out on the brink of the white water. Death was there, breathing over him and calling him, but big Careless had secured foothold on the very ledge of the first cataract and once more moved towards the shore.

30

That firmer footing lifted him higher. In a moment he had whipped Sleeper out of the creek and through the brush on the farther bank. The jaws of Sleeper could relax their hold at last.

When he staggered to his feet, he could see the silhouette of a rider moving up and down the farther bank of the stream opposite the cataract, as though searching the flow of the currents for a last sight of Sleeper's body. It was not strange if he had not been able to make out the incredible rescue. Then the rider turned his horse back into the woods. He would go now, to keep that appointment for which he was late—that meeting with Kate Williams; what other woman would he have in mind at this time?

Sleeper, stepping back against a boulder, fumbled till he found a sharp edge of the rock and then chafed against it the cords which bound his wrists. His hands were free in a moment, free to caress the noble head of Careless, who stood dripping and trembling from his work.

Then into the wet saddle Sleeper swung himself. He put the stallion into that long striding gallop which jerked the trees away into the darkness that flowed like a river to the rear.

Loder, with over a hundred thousand dollars in his hands after that "fifty-fifty split," was going at his ease across country on the horse of his dead partner. How long would it take Sleeper to reach the old shack east of White Water town and give the word to Pop Lowry?

That was on the way to the Williams ranch. There would not be time, also, to ride into White Water and raise a crowd of fighting men to head towards the ranch. Men most likely would say that the loafer was crazy, out of his head. And in the meantime, Loder would be keeping his appointment with the girl, and taking her away to the unknown place where there was waiting a "fellow who looked enough like a minister to suit anybody."

He, Sleeper, would have to get out there and prevent the catastrophe—he, with his empty hands!

The big horse blew through the upper ravines like the wind, struck the lower valley. But the lights of White Water were far, far ahead when Sleeper turned aside down a lane which was almost overgrown with brush. He came out into a clearing where the bushes moved like waves against the moldering little shack. There was a light inside. It showed in pale streaks through the cracks between the boards.

"Lowry!" shouted Sleeper.

He swung from the back of the stallion as he spoke. The door of the shack yawned wide, and in the entrance stood the tall, bent form of the peddler. He lifted the lantern in order to throw light on the form of Sleeper, and so doing, he illumined the gleaming baldness of his own head.

"Hello, Sleeper," said Lowry. "Damn my old eyes—is that Careless you got with you?"

"They didn't go to Chimney Creek," panted Sleeper.

"I know that—now!" said Lowry. "Doggone me, but I listened to lies. I was takin' a long chance."

"At a hundred and ten thousand dollars, eh?" snapped Sleeper.

Lowry whistled. "As much as that?" said he. And he made a clucking sound of surprise. "Where's Belling?"

"Dead—murdered—and chewed to bits in the White Water cataracts."

The calm rejoinder of the peddler was merely: "You look kind of wet yourself, Sleeper."

"Loder killed him," said Sleeper.

"That ain't a big surprise to me. So Loder has the whole bunch of the money, now?"

"Lowry, you're not working a lone hand—you've got men with you—how many?"

"Why, I wouldn't know, exactly," said Lowry. "There's

lots of good men to be hired, here and there."

"Listen—Loder has gone to the Williams ranch. I'm a dead man. I mean, he thinks that I'm dead. I tell you, he has more than a hundred thousand dollars on him. Lowry, if you have ways of doing things, do them now. Can you get men to the Williams place or do I have to go into White Water and try to raise a crowd?"

"Don't raise no crowd, brother!" said Lowry. "Crowd's ain't any good. For a feller like Loder, every crowd is too doggone big in the mesh and he just slips away into the brush again. I'll handle Loder—"

He pulled something from his pocket and blew a whistle that screamed across the night and seemed to draw a train of fire through the brain of Sleeper.

"You can have all the cash," said Sleeper. "But get there with your men, Pop. There's been murder already, tonight, and there's going to be something worse unless we're fast."

He threw himself back into the saddle.

"Wait a minute! Where you going?"

"To the Williams ranch."

"Not alone. Sleeper, listen, you fool! You'll spoil the whole idea—"

But Sleeper was already gone, bending low in the saddle as he shot the stallion among the trees with the branches whishing overhead.

He crossed the valley with big Careless running still at top speed. He passed through the gap in the hills and, coming out on the wide plateau beyond, was aware of the faint glimmering of lights ahead of him.

That was the Williams ranch.

6

Even the mighty endurance of Careless was sapped before he brought his rider to the Williams ranch house. He stopped very willingly under the trees and dropped his head to wheeze for fresh breath while Sleeper made for the first light. It shone from the windows of the big living room. Long, Spanish windows, from floor to ceiling, that could be opened up to turn the room into an outdoors place in effect. The night was warm and the windows were open now. Sleeper could see Kate Williams dressed in riding clothes as brown as her suntanned skin. She was reading on a couch. The light from the nearest lamp cast a curving brightness across her and left half of her in shadow.

Over his shoulder, Sleeper glanced this way and that. He could thank God that the girl was there but now that he had found her, he wanted other people on hand. She looked suddenly up as though she had felt his glance touching her. Then she sprang to her feet with a cry.

He knew the picture that he must be making, even in the dimness by the window. One sleeve was ripped away, and the brush through which Careless had dragged him had left many a rip in the old clothes. Besides, he had dried only to a general dampness which made the ragged clothes cling close to him.

"It's all right!" he said. "Nothing to worry you."

"It's Sleeper!" she said. "Why, Sleeper, come in—I mean, what do you want?"

"Nothing at all," said he. "I'd like to see your father, or the rest of the men—"

"Father's gone to bed. And all the hands have gone off to the fiesta. Why, Sleeper? What do you want?"

34

"They've all gone?" he echoed, feeling as though there was doom around him.

Williams himself, elderly, and cursed with a perpetual tremor of the hands—why, he would be worse than useless in the trouble that was sure to come.

There was nothing to pray for except the coming of Lowry and Lowry's men. Could he be sure that Lowry *had* men? Had that blast on the whistle meant something real?

"There's something wrong," said the girl. "Do tell me what it is. I was so sorry today, when you almost got Careless for your own horse. Sleeper, tell me what's the trouble."

"No trouble for me," he answered, stepping a short distance into the room. "But a lot of trouble ahead for you, Kate, I'm afraid."

She raised a hand suddenly to her face and peered at him. "Trouble?" she echoed. "For me?"

"Loder," said he.

The blow struck her hard. He looked vaguely over the big, barnlike room. What could he do except strike her again.

"Do you mean—?" she began.

"I know about it," he said. "I know the way you feel, too. That Charlie Loder has had a bad deal. That he's as good a man, really, as can be found."

"That *is* the truth!" she exclaimed.

"It's not the truth," said Sleeper. "I've seen him kill a man tonight—shoot him in the back."

He could see the words hurt her like a striking hand. Then she tossed up her head and drew in a great breath.

"Sleeper," she said. "that's a slander—and a lie!"

"Is it?" said Sleeper, his pride not in the least hurt. "I'll name the man he killed—Belling."

"A thief and a man-killer! Everyone knows what Belling is!"

"Was!" said he. "Belling's dead, and the cataracts of

35

the White Water have chewed him up small and fine."

"Then—if Charlie had a hand in it, he had to strike in self-defense!" she declared.

He admired, in a strange way, this faith which she had lodged so invincibly in the outlaw. "You can see that my own clothes are a little wet," he said.

"I can see that," she answered, white-faced, frowning.

"I had to jump into the White Water to get away from Charlie Loder's gun," he said. "I had to jump—with my hands tied behind me."

"Sleeper! But—your hands tied behind you?"

"Yes."

"Above the cataract?"

He could see the direction in which her thought was moving.

"A horse saved me—Careless."

"A horse saved you!" she cried, utterly incredulous.

"He came for me, and I grabbed the stirrup with my teeth. Careless pulled me out. He's out there now— Careless—if you want to see him."

"Isn't it the truth that you've *stolen* Careless?" she exclaimed, "and if Charlie did anything—it was to a horse-thief?"

Outside the house a very thin and musical whistle sounded. The girl started, turned suddenly towards the sound.

"I—" she began. "I'll talk to you—later, Sleeper!"

"You can't go to Loder," he answered.

"How do you dare to say that?" she demanded.

"He's got a fellow who looks like a minister to marry you. But it's not a real minister. He's got a real gold ring for you, and that's the only truth in what he's going to do. Will you believe me?"

"I'll never believe you!" cried the girl.

"You've got to," answered he. "I've only got seconds left, and if Loder finds me here, he'll prove what he is —by murdering me, Kate."

The thin whistle sounded again, a good deal closer.

"I've got to go!" exclaimed the girl. "There can't be a word of truth in what you've said."

"Well, then," said he, "I'll play my last card. It probably won't be worth a thing, either." He took from inside his shirt the bit of oiled silk and drew from it the picture. Only at the edges was it wet.

"Did you know that Charlie Loder was a married man?" he asked.

She came swiftly and snatched the picture. There was no great need of question and examination. The white veil and the pretty face of the girl, the flowers in her hand, and tall Charlie Loder standing beside her—that was the story quickly enough.

"Then it's someone that he married a long time ago," she stammered. "Years and years, and she's dead—or they're divorced—"

"Does he look a lot younger in that picture?" asked Sleeper.

The girl, with a moan, slipped into the depths of a chair and lay there with her head far back, the picture trailing from one hand towards the floor. And Sleeper looked away from her to find tall Charlie Loder on the farther side of the room.

The girl saw him, too. She sprang up, crying, "It isn't true, Charlie! I know it isn't true!"

Loder, disregarding her utterly, made a sufficient answer. He kept a steady, deadly eye on Sleeper and drew a revolver from beneath his coat.

7

Loder would not miss. Men said that he *could* not miss. It was three steps to reach the tall window and the dark of the night outside it. Even if only one step had been needed, it would have been too much.

Sleeper rested the finger tips of his right hand on the table beside him. There was a heavy little Mexican ashtray made of iron lying on the table, and that would be his only weapon.

The girl said nothing, did nothing. She only stood there holding out the picture like a statue.

"Careless pulled you through, did he?" said Loder. "Well, you've had all the luck that's going to be with you on one night. You're going to die, Sleeper!"

"No!" screamed the girl. "Charlie, you won't murder him!"

"Stop the yapping, you little yellow-headed fool," snarled Loder. "If I'd had a chance to get you, I would have made some dough out of that wooden-headed father of yours. But the kid smashed my game! By God, when I think of it, I don't believe it's true. I'm dreaming, here, and Sleeper's where he ought to be, in hell with Belling."

His voice went crazy—it fell to pieces in a screech: "Take this—you slinking snake!"

Sleeper snatched at the iron ashtray as he ducked. He seemed to be bowing to fate, but he dipped so low that the bullet which should have smashed through his ribs and his heart only slashed his back.

He sidestepped like a boxer—and ran in.

A fellow who flees merely steadies the nerves of the enemy. But no man in the world is perfectly cool against a charge. Sleeper had just about one thousandth of a second to do this thinking, and that was time enough.

He hurled that heavy little iron tray as he dodged in. The second bullet brushed his face with hornet wings. And the tray clipped the side of Loder's head as he fired the third shot. The bullet went into the wooden floor as Sleeper dived at his man.

The life of Sleeper had been rich in time; God had given him an eye faster than an antelope's heels—and now he was fighting for his life. He had a thirty pound handicap of hard muscle to overcome—plus a gun.

He got rid of the gun first, when Sleeper, with the edge of his hand, struck the gun-hand of Loder at the wrist.

The fingers of Loder opened as though on springs. The heavy Colt crashed on the floor and spun away.

That made the right hand of Loder not much good for the instant. With the left he dropped a heavy blow behind Sleeper's ear. The weight of it and the stunning impact flattened him on the floor.

He had a chance to see Loder reaching for the fallen Colt. He saw the girl, too. She had picked up a heavy poker from the fireplace, and she was running in with the long iron poised above her head in both hands. Her face was contorted out of all human semblance. She was white—a sort of stone or pale clay color. And she was screaming continually: "Murder! Murder! Murder!"

Half the brain of Sleeper was numb but he had wit enough to use his feet where his hands could not help him. He kicked with his heel at Loder's knee and saw the big fellow slither to the floor. Sleeper, with a turn of his entire body, with a leap like that of a snake, was at his man at once.

A fist cracked him between the eyes. He got hold of that arm and gave it a sudden twist. Loder howled. They rolled over. Sleeper twisted that arm again and heard the cracking, muffled sounds of breaking bones. The scream of Loder was a frightful thing.

Then something flashed. It was the revolver, which Loder had scooped up from the floor with his right hand.

Sleeper swayed his head to the side. That was not enough to avoid the coming blow. He felt the thud of it. The butt of the gun seemed to crash straight through against his brain. He could see and hear, dimly, but his body was asleep.

Loder was on his feet. He knocked the iron rod out of the hands of the screaming girl and as it was flung away, he struck her backhanded with the barrel of the gun. She fell on her knees.

The screaming had ended. It had been like a fire, enwrapping Sleeper's half-numbed brain. Now he was able to think, and he knew that he was about to die.

The left arm of Loder swayed uncertainly, crookedly. But his right hand was steady enough, holding the gun. His face was old, knotted and twisted by an agony and by hate as though by decades of foul life.

"And so this is the answer, eh?" he said.

Footfalls were hurrying down from the top part of the house.

"I'd like to take time on you," said Loder. "But I've got to hurry. By God, I'd like to take my time. I'd like to have the blonde-headed little fool awake to watch me, too."

The girl lay on her face, senseless. Sleeper propped himself up on his hands to face the bullet.

"Right between the eyes is the surest place, Loder," he said.

Then a voice behind Loder said from one of the big open windows: "This way, Charlie!"

Loder jerked his head around over his shoulder while his gun still covered Sleeper.

There was a stocky man with unshaven red beard on his face. There was a very tall, very thin man with a foolish grin. There was a third fellow, who was Pop Lowry, the peddler. Two of them had revolvers, but old Pop carried a leveled rifle. And all three guns spoke at once.

The weight of the driving lead turned Loder. He struck on his side and, turning on his back, lay dead beside Sleeper. Perhaps it was the impact of the fall that made a living sigh pass through his lips.

"And the kid?" said the unshaven man, calmly.

"Leave him alone! He's saved the stuff for us!" commanded Lowry.

It was Pop Lowry who reached the fallen body of big Loder first. There was no searching to be done. Both coat pockets were bulging with the packages of money. Pop Lowry got it, turned, and fled. For the footfalls of Williams were rapidly approaching the room.

They kept Sleeper for a whole week in the Williams house, though he was ready to ride on the third day. But, since he was in a ground-floor room, and since there was a bit of pasture right behind the house, he was able to lie propped up in the bed and look through the window at Careless, grazing in the sun.

Two or three times a day he would whistle, and Careless, leaping the fence, came and thrust his head in through the window. He could reach the bed of his master, and he did this with a great deal of care, snuffing loudly in protest against the smell of the iodine. Only when he had his velvet muzzle right against the hand of Sleeper would he be sure that it was indeed the master.

Then there was the rancher, who used to come in several times a day and spend hours chatting. He brought reports of how his daughter was convalescing during her sickness. The nerve shock had been very great, but the doc declared that in a few weeks she would be able to travel.

41

"And now for you," said Williams, on the seventh day. "I want to make your future my charge, Sleeper. I want you to pick out the thing you wish to do; and then I'll see that you have the means to do it. I don't care what the scale is. What you've saved me from—what you've saved Kate from, to put it better—"

Sleeper frowned at the ceiling.

"I want to thank you," he said, "but—"

"Don't let there be any 'buts,'" urged Williams.

"We'll remember each other kindly, and let it go at that," said Sleeper.

"My dear fellow—" began Williams.

But Sleeper shook his head in such a way that the rancher understood argument would do no good.

This, perhaps, was a greater shock to Williams than anything had ever happened in his life, including that terrible scene in his living room when he had found a wounded man on the floor beside a dead man, and his daughter senseless, nearby.

"We want to forget this, anyway," said Sleeper. "All that people know is that Loder came to your house, to rob it, maybe. And that Sleeper happened to be going by and got drawn into the thing—nobody knows exactly how. And that some enemies of Loder had followed him and murdered him in the house. That's all people know. It's all that's good for them to know. If they wonder why I've got Careless—well, they can ask Shorty Joe Bennett to explain, if they can find Shorty—"

Things were left like that. And when Sleeper left the Williams house on the seventh day, he rode Careless not to the town of White Water but to the little shack abandoned in the woods to the east of the town. He found the peddler with glasses on his big nose, sitting in long red underwear on a stump and sewing a patch on the seat of an old pair of trousers.

Pop Lowry looked up from threading a needle and

then pushed his glasses high up on his forehead. "Well, well, well!" he said. "I been waiting for you all of these days. And here you are!"

"Here I am for pay day," said Sleeper.

"Pay day?" exclaimed the peddler in great surprise. "You got Careless, didn't you? Ain't he worth more than the thousand dollars I was gonna give you?"

Sleeper smiled kindly down at Pop Lowry. "Look here, Pop," he said. "I did a few things more than you asked me to do."

"That's me," said Lowry. "I always throw in enough to make folks satisfied, over and above what they pay for."

"I've given you more than a thousand dollars' worth of silence," said Sleeper. "Suppose that I let people know that Pop Lowry has just collected at least half of a hundred and ten thousand dollars? Suppose I let them know that he had hold of Belling—and let him get away? Suppose I let them know that Pop Lowry only has to blow a whistle and a crowd of gunmen come out of the woods? Wouldn't they wonder why Pop keeps on wandering around through the mountains with his three mules?"

Pop Lowry sighed. "How come that you never done any talking, Sleeper?" he asked.

He drew a purse from his pocket and took almost all the bills that were in it. These he passed to Sleeper. "I would of thought," said Lowry, "that you'd of wanted to make a hero out of yourself, Sleeper. You've done enough to sit high the rest of your life, if you only talked a little."

"People that sit up high can't whittle a stick and enjoy the sunshine," said Sleeper.

The peddler laughed. "You're a queer one, Sleeper," he said. "You gonna go right on, the same old way?"

"Are you going to keep packing your mules and selling

43

stuff cheap—because you've got no overhead, Pop?" countered Sleeper.

The peddler scratched his chin and finally permitted himself a very broad smile. Sleeper was smiling, also.

8

Something was wrong. Sleeper had noticed nothing unusual from the higher land, but as soon as he reached the low ground beside Crazy Horse Creek, he felt a tremor through the earth and a quivering in the air, or was it only a tension in his own nerves, a sudden, inexplicable warning that freighted the hot midday—a thing of the mind rather than the body?

He slipped from the back of the bright chestnut stallion. He looked in his ragged, patched rig, like some vagabond grub-line rider who might have stolen the great horse. Now, rising in his stirrups and scanning the horizon on all sides, he saw nothing at all.

On the edge of the horizon towards White Water there was a small cloud. Otherwise the sky was a clear basalt blue. The sound that he had heard or felt, could it be thunder rolling from that small cloud so near the horizon? He shook his head, brow puckering. No sense to that. Yet, there *was* something. . . .

He stretched himself flat on the earth and pressed his ear to it. There was no vibration, no sound transmitted. The golden chestnut put down his head anxiously, and snuffed at the ground beside his master. Sleeper caught

44

him by the mane and so was swept to his feet as the stallion tossed his head. He continued that movement, with a slight spring that brought him right into the saddle. Then he rode Careless straight into the creek.

The stallion had seemed perfectly unconcerned while it was on dry ground, but as soon as it entered the water it showed every sign of fear, flattening its ears and looking repeatedly towards the bend of the creek, upstream.

"What the devil's the matter, Careless?" asked Sleeper.

The horse rolled his bright eyes back as though he wished to make answer, and at the same time pressed forward across the stream. The stallion was well into the middle, the current sweeping up about the glossy shoulders, when a change of the wind blew a definite sound of thunder towards Sleeper. And then a moment later, looking upstream, he saw the cause of it.

A wall of water six feet high was sweeping around the bend. It was almost as straight as masonry, excepting for its angry yellow foam on top and the tree trunks and debris tumbling there, and thousands of tons of lunging current pushed behind it. It had not made enough noise to send its voice before it against the wind, but now that the air changed it sent a sound like the distant thunder of a trail herd's hoofs. It was as though nature, like a murderer, knife in hand, had crept up behind her victim and was now in leaping distance, ready to strike.

Veering about the curve, that wall of water sheered off the bank as though with the stroke of a vast shovel. Some big cottonwoods were jerked down into the currents, buried. One of them leaped up again, showing all its length like a living thing that strove to escape from torture.

The wave came fast. Far away in the hills a cloudburst must have dropped into the upper valley and now its burden was rushing softly through the lower land.

Now that it had appeared, as though casting all caution to the wind, it shouted aloud. So a lion might roar as it leaps for the kill, paralyzing every sense in the helpless prey. So a grizzly thunders as it rises to strike down a prime beeve.

But Sleeper was not paralyzed. He cast one look behind him toward the bank which he had left. The distance behind him was greater than that which lay ahead. Also, time would be lost in the turning. So he called to Careless through the tumult, and the stallion lunged furiously ahead. He must have sensed the danger from afar, and now he fought with a human eagerness for his life and that of his master.

If it had been all shallow water, he would have rushed through to the safety of the farther shore. Instead, he was plunged, swimming, into water higher than his head.

Sleeper, slipping instantly into the stream, swam powerfully beside him. He could have gained on the stallion and reached the shore in safety, perhaps, but he had no thought of that. He would as soon have thought of abandoning a portion of his own body as of leaving Careless behind him.

And in the meantime the wave rushed on them. It was sweeping closer. Already a strange tremor broke the surface of the creek into a tiny dance of waves. They would be caught; they would be hurled down the stream. And now, over the head of the wall of water, Sleeper saw the heavy butt of a tree trunk lifting, lurching toward him. A fall from a cliff could not have given more certain promise of death.

Then—it was not that he heard the shouting of the man's voice through the tumult, but because an instinct made him look up—Sleeper saw a horseman on the bank toward which he struggled. A lean man of the desert on a desert mustang, all rawhide and bones. And the stranger was swinging a rope, ready for the cast.

Sleeper, with a waved arm, gave signal that he was

ready. The rope shot out, landed in Sleeper's grasp and the noose was instantly over the horn of the saddle.

"Not the horse, you fool! I can't pull the horse in— too heavy—grab the rope for yourself!" shouted the rider.

But Sleeper, though he heard the voice faintly and clearly now, did not change his mind or the grip of the rope.

They would live together or die together, he and Careless. And now he saw the towering face of the wall of dull water high above him. The uproar grew immense. And on the shore the rider pulling his horse back on its haunches to receive the pull, was taking a dally around the saddle horn, ready to turn it loose if the strain threatened to engulf him and his pony in the swirling cascade.

The rope caught hard on Careless' pommel. His head came upstream. Struggling with all his might, the force of the stream now helped to sway him with the strain of the lariat towards the shore. He had hoofs on the shoaling ground when the edge of the rolling wall struck him and rolled him. Sleeper, casting himself ahead, gripped the rope just before the nose of the stallion and rolled with him in the same terrible confusion.

The sky flashed over his head; was lost; flashed again as he bit at the air for life-giving breath. The rope trembled with the frightful strain. The trunk of a small tree leaped past him like a dark snake.

And then, in an instant the danger was gone, and they were drawn from the edge of the monstrous wave up on the high, dry bank. There the desert rider calmly began to pull in his loosened rope and methodically coil it. Water had swept as high as the shoulders of his mustang. Now that the peril was past, he seemed as calm as though he had done no more than rope a calf at the branding pen.

And Careless, safe at last, unharmed, polished to a

47

burning copper with water and sunlight, turned and sent a great neigh of defiance after the rush of the wave.

That wall of water was speeding fast down the valley. It turned the curve below and the thunder of it was gone. There was only the sloshing sound of the following water, and the noise of sucking as the dry sand drank up the stream.

Sleeper shook some of the water from him and went up to the stranger. The man was sunburned till his face was leather-dark, and his faded eyebrows were only pale marks against the skin. There seemed to be a permanent dust settled in the wrinkles about the eyes and the mouth. A face as long and lean as the body of the man; a tired face; but the eyes were filled with restless life.

Sleeper held out his hand. "Thanks," he said.

His hand was taken in a dry, quick grasp. The palm of the stranger felt like a rough paper. "That's all right, kid," he said. "One of them near things though."

"We'd be dead as hell if you hadn't stuck to your place," remarked Sleeper beginning to strip off his soaking clothes.

"That horse belong to you?" asked the stranger, running his glance over the matchless lines of the great stallion. "Or you taking it some place for your boss?"

"Taking it some place for my boss," said Sleeper. "Only I'm the boss." He smiled and explained, "I've got a claim on Careless, but he's got a claim on me, too."

"Yeah?" drawled the man. "What's your name, kid?"

"Sleeper."

"Bones is what most of the boys call me," volunteered the rider. "What price would you put on that horse?"

"I'm not selling him."

"Better put a price on him," urged Bones. "He'd be useful to a man in a pinch. And I'm that man."

"Not selling," said Sleeper shortly.

He had his clothes off, now, and began to wring them.

Dressed, he looked as though he would strip as lean as a plucked crow. Instead, the rounded depth of his chest was a surprise, and his arms and legs were round, also, with an intricate rippling of lithe muscles. Every part of his body had the supple strength of a cat's forearm. But the glance of Bones was for the horse, not for the man.

"Kid," he said, "I wouldn't want to beat you down. I'd pay five hundred for a horse like that."

"He's been sold for a thousand," said Sleeper.

Bones flushed. "I'm paying five hundred," he said. "Maybe I'll send you some more later on."

"Thanks," said Sleeper, "but he's not being sold."

"The mustang and five hundred bucks," said Bones in a low voice.

He dismounted and went to the head of Careless. "I'm sorry, Sleeper," said Bones. "But I need a good horse, right now. I got a real need for him."

"I'd lend him to you till you're through the pinch," said Sleeper.

"Lending be damned. I want to own him. Here's the money. Take that or take nothing!"

9

Sleeper, stretching out his hand for the money, laid his grasp lightly on the wrist of Bones. And by that touch he read the whole body of the tall man. There might be a hundred and eighty pounds in that bony frame and by the stiffness of the tendons in the wrist he was muscled like a mule. Not an ounce of fat existed on him. He was tough as rawhide all the way through.

"Too bad, mister," said Sleeper. "I'm not selling."

"You poor fool!" answered Bones. "Then you get the mustang—an' that's all!"

He tried to pull away the hand containing the money, but the grasp of Sleeper held it. "Why—damn you!" cried Bones, jerking.

He had a gun at his hip but he didn't try to use it against this unarmed kid. Instead, he tried a blow which had begun and ended many a fight for him in the line camp, bunkhouse, and trail-town brawl wherever he had traveled on the rough way of his life. It was a neat, chopping, overhand right that would glide over a man's guard and drop like the blow of a loaded whip-butt on the jaw. Now, because he was impatient, he forgot the slightness of the figure of this younger man and lashed out with his full strength.

Very slightly Sleeper shifted. The crushing blow brushed the skin of his cheek, and seemed to spin him about. His left hand, reaching up like the dart of a snake's head as he turned his back on Bones, caught the striking fist at the wrist and pulled it down over his shoulder. Then he doubled over and Bones' lanky weight shot into the air, landed on the sand in a rolling fall.

The mustang tossed its head and ran a short distance away. The golden stallion came closer with bright, inquisitive eyes. But Bones did not rise at once. He lay flat on his back, stunned, and stared at the sun, while Sleeper removed the six-gun from its holster. Then he reached inside the loose of the man's flannel shirt for the braided strands of horsehair from which there was suspended a small double-barrelled derringer. He took it.

After that, he stepped back and sat down on a rock and tossed both guns a little distance away onto the sand.

When Bones sat up, he found Sleeper playing with a

50

hunting knife which he was tossing into the air, and catching by the point on his thumb-nail as the knife whirled down. It was a heavy knife and the point of it was so thin that it was a mere streak of light. The clothes had been spread out to dry on the rock beside Sleeper.

"Where'd you learn that trick?" asked Bones, without grudge or passion.

"I know a Chinaman up in the hills," said Sleeper. "He's pretty nearly fifty, but he's still faster than a flash with his hands. He does queer things. You grab him and he makes your own weight beat you. I've worked for years with him."

He yawned and stretched, letting the knife sink point down into the sand, so that only the tip of its handle appeared above the surface.

"When I'm not trying his tricks, I'm thinking about them," he said. "Tricks like his take a whole lot of thinking."

Finding his clothes were drying too slowly, he shook them out in the sun again. Bones rose and rolled a cigarette. "You're a better man than I am—with your hands," he said calmly.

"Sorry," said Sleeper. "But I knew the sand was pretty soft and would break the fall. Otherwise it would have snapped your left shoulder, maybe."

"You mean that you've really worked out this game till you know what will happen every lick of the time?"

"Pretty much. I don't know as much as old Sam Wu, but I know something. He still has a lot to teach me, but I keep on learning."

"I'd like to take some wrestling lessons from him," said Bones.

"It's not wrestling. It's a way of living, too. You have to learn to stand pain and look as though you like it. That's one of the things that you have to start when you're pretty young. They teach you to relax." Sleeper

51

grinned and stretched and yawned again. "That's the lesson that I learned the best," he said.

Bones rubbed his left shoulder thoughtfully. "I've missed something," he muttered.

"I told you before that you could have Careless for a loan," said Sleeper. "Why don't you take him? He'll carry you clean away from the sheriff."

"Who said anything about the sheriff?" asked Bones.

"Well, the dead men didn't tell me," said Sleeper, smiling. "Neither of them said a word."

Bones, growing slightly pale, took a stealthy step forward.

"It's all right," said Sleeper. "I'm no bounty hunter, I don't want blood money."

"By God!" exclaimed Bones, "they couldn't have posted the reward this far away, as quick as all this!"

"They didn't post any reward."

"How d'you know—I mean—damn it, kid, who are you, anyway?"

"I'm a friend," said Sleeper, with a sudden gravity. He rose and held out his hand. Bones took it with a gingerly grasp.

"All right," he said.

"Say the same thing to me," went on Sleeper, "and you're welcome to those guns."

Bones hesitated for an instant. The word was apparently an important one to him, but finally he muttered: "*Bueno*, we're friends. And damned if this don't beat me."

"Come along," said Sleeper. "You ought to be on your way, and we'll talk while we ride. You won't take Careless?"

Bones pulled out a bandanna and wiped his forehead. "I need to make miles," he said, "but if I borrow Careless, you'll never see him again.

"He owes you his life and I owe you mine," said Sleeper.

"It was only when you said that you were going to *take* him that I couldn't stand it."

"I was buying him."

"A million wouldn't buy Careless. But can you ride him? Some can't."

"I'll try him." He stalked to the place where his guns lay, picked them up, and blew the sand out of them. Then he put them away. Once, as he handled the weapons, he cast a grim glance towards Sleeper. Then he went to the golden stallion.

"It's the first time in my life that I ever took something for nothing," he said.

"You're welcome," said Sleeper. He took a great breath and looked down at the ground.

"What's his style?" asked Bones.

Sleeper had to pause before he could force himself to answer. "He'll do a little fence-rowing," he answered. "Then he's likely to sunfish. And sometimes he falls over backward, and gets up with a jump. But the worst part is—that he'll start whirling anytime. And come out of the whirl by throwing himself at the ground and flopping over sideways."

"My God," said Bones, "how does *anybody* ride him? And where did he learn all those tricks?"

"I've been teaching him a little," Sleeper admitted. "But maybe he can be ridden still. Wait a minute."

He went up to the stallion, took the hand of Bones, and laid it between the eyes of the stallion. "Here's a friend, Careless," he said. "Be good to him. Take it easy and give him a chance."

Still holding the hand of Bones, he sleeked the neck of the horse with it. The ears of Careless flicked forward but flattened against his skull again, giving his fine head an ominously snaky look.

"That's about all I can do for you, partner," said Sleeper, "Try him now."

53

The puzzled eyes of Bones dwelt for an instant on the face of his companion. "It's worse than hell for you to give him up, ain't it?" he asked. "Well, If I can manage it, he'll come back to you when I'm through the pinch."

"Thanks," said Sleeper briefly. He stood at the head of the stallion, his hand against the muzzle of the great horse until Bones had mounted. Then he stepped back.

Careless rose from the earth like a disembodied flag of fire. Like the tossing of flame he began to soar and smite the ground, and soar again.

He went over backward. Big Bones, flinging himself clear, barely managed to leap into the saddle again as Careless sprang up. But he was not yet settled in the stirrups when the stallion began to spin. Vainly Bones tried to right himself in the saddle. His body sloped more and more out to the side. He would certainly have been hurled like a stone from a sling if the voice of the master had not shouted, suddenly. And, at that, Careless came to a snorting, stamping halt, throwing up his head, shuddering his skin in a vast desire to shake this unwanted burden from his back.

Bones slipped at once to the ground.

"No good," he admitted, "There's more tricks in that big silky devil than there is in any tinhorn's deck. How did you teach him this stuff?"

"I used to tie a sack of dirt on his back—tie it with twine and then make him do the tricks to throw it off. Besides, he knows some stuff of his own. I'm afraid that I've taught him too well."

Bones went to his mustang and mounted. "Come along with me," he said. "Talking won't make the miles any longer that lie ahead of this mustang."

They climbed to the higher ground, and jogging toward the hills, Bones picked out the mouth of a ravine.

"D'you want to go down that valley?" asked Sleeper, curiously. "I wouldn't, if I were you."

"Why not?"

"You'll be bottled up inside it."

"It's the quickest way through the hills—unless the gents have come out of White Water and started hunting for me. I dunno how they could of got word, though. It's a long ways off from where I had my trouble. But how did *you* know about me?"

"About what?"

"You knew there was a sheriff after me. Who told you that?"

"Sheriffs usually head up a man-hunt."

"Well, but you talked about dead men. About two dead men!"

"There wouldn't be one man. Anybody that knew you well enough to risk a gunfight with you would want to have a partner. If there were more than two, you'd probably get out of the way. If there were two, you'd likely fight it out. And if you fought, you'd be likely to kill. But it's just mostly guessing, about the two men."

"Kid, can I talk to you?"

"I'll tell you this," said Sleeper, "any trouble you get into, from now on, is my trouble, too."

A sneer began to form on the face of the other, but it disappeared at once.

"I've always been ready to play my hand against the world, Sleeper," he said. "But you're different, I can see that. A fellow that chucks away his chances and stays with his horse is a lot different from the rest of the world. All the way through you're different. But how did you know about the price on me?"

Sleeper looked at him and smiled. "Once I took a trail herd to Denver," he said. "After I played the town, I struck one place that had a hawk and an eagle—caged, they were. They had the same look in their eye that you have. They'd only been caught for a couple of weeks . . . You've raised quite a lot of hell in your time, Bones."

55

Bones squinted at the distant horizon and then sighed. "Yeah, I've raised my share of hell and now it's ready to burn me," he said. "But I've never been a killer, Sleeper. McGregor and Loftus, they needed a leadin' bad, and they got it."

"As how?" asked Sleeper.

"They did the grub-staking. I located the mine. They knew who I was. They knew that I was going straight —that I *had* gone straight for years. And they said that the past didn't matter with them, that they'd trust me, so I staked a claim. Free gold in quartz—the prettiest stuff you ever seen. They went out and had a look, McGregor and Loftus did, then they tried to make a big double-cross. If they turned me over to the law, I'd be lost, they'd get the mine, and I'd never see my half of it. You see? They jumped me in the middle of the night, with guns. But I had the luck, I left them both, and I left them dead. But now I'm on the trail again, and God knows where it'll end! That's my story, kid."

"It's a true story," said Sleeper. "You're sure you want to ride down this old bottle-necked ravine?"

"It's the short cut, Sleeper. Nobody around these parts is likely to know the law is after me with a price on my head. You only guessed it."

"Well—maybe it's the short cut, but I don't like it," answered Sleeper.

"Because you can afford to take the long way around—you with a horse under you that's as good as a pair of wings. But I've got to save miles. Pardner, they've put ten thousand dollars on my head!"

Sleeper translated the money into different terms, saying aloud: "Suppose that a puncher works like the devil and saves twenty a month. Four years to a thousand. Forty years to ten thousand. Why, the price on you is as much as a cattleman could save in a whole life-time. And the hills are going to be full of men looking for you, Bones!"

"All right. Let 'em try to find me!" snapped Bones.

10

They entered the mouth of the long ravine. It wound back into the hills, with the walls rising higher and higher and more precipitous ever moment. Here and there were narrow cut-backs into the hills, but often for a mile at a time, there was no chance to dodge to the right or to the left.

Bones, loosening the rifle in its saddle holster, sometimes looked up anxiously to the walls of the ravine, and then set his jaw the harder.

"Luck," he said. "There ain't anything but luck that a gent like me can pray for. Luck, and a good horse, and a gun that won't miss."

"You know what Sam Wu would advise you to do?"

"The Chink who teaches you the wrestling? What would he tell me to do?"

"Empty your guns, or throw them away."

"And give away my last chance?"

"He'd say that a chance to kill is not a chance worth having."

"Are you nutty, Sleeper? D'you believe what you're saying?"

"I try to believe it," said Sleeper. "Sam Wu—he's the one who keeps me from—well, he keeps me from being foolish a good many times."

"Listen!" exclaimed Bones. He lifted a quick hand. "You hear it?" he asked.

"No. What is it?"

"Now you can hear it. A horse coming this way, fast."

Sleeper could finally make out the distant beating of the hoofs over the rocks and the earth, now clear, now muffled. And now around the next bend of the ravine came a rider full tilt, the horse swaying to a slant as it took the turn at full speed.

In a moment, the stranger was waving a hand high in the air. Big Bones pulled in his horse with a grunt.

"A friend!" he said. "I didn't know that I had any friends up here!"

The rider came on very fast towards the halted pair.

"Bad news!" muttered Bones. "Good news would never come as fast as all of that!"

"It's a girl!" exclaimed Sleeper.

She was dressed like a man from sombrero to boots; she was as slim and straight as a boy, too. But the touch of the wind showed a body softer than that of a man and as the brim of the sombrero flared up in the wind of the gallop, Sleeper could see the small face and the brightness of it.

She skidded her pinto to a halt. "Hello, Bones!" she called, stretching out her hand.

"Hello, Maisry," he answered. "Doggone your blue eyes, but I'm glad to see you. What you doin' up here?"

"Who's that?" snapped the girl, looking straight with those blue eyes at Sleeper. And he saw the sleek of her black hair beneath her hat. She was dark as an Indian, almost; with that black hair she might have been an Indian indeed, but the blue of the eyes told a different story.

"Calls himself Sleeper," explained Bones. "He's on the inside with me. What's the bad news?"

"Bad as hell," said the girl. "I hit White Water with the Colonel, and—"

"The Colonel up here, too?" cried Bones.

"Be still while I tell you. You've got to hump, Bones. The first thing we ran into was news about you. They say that both McGregor and Loftus are dead. And you did it."

"Sure," said Bones calmly.

58

"I knew that hell would bust out of you," said the girl. "This hombre is all right, is he?" She jerked her head toward Sleeper.

"Sure. He's inside. How could that news hit White Water?"

"They pushed a relay through; rode night and day. The whole doggone town is cut loose into the hills. They know that you're headed this way. They know that you're worth ten thousand dollars, dead or alive. Bones, what a wooden-head you were to knock over McGregor and Loftus! You've got to turn back!"

Bones looked over his shoulder. "If I turn back into the flat country, I'll run straight into the bunch that's coming up from the south," he said.

"We'll cut aside," said Sleeper. "They think you're headed north. We'll cut straight to the east. And ride like the devil!"

"That's sense," said the girl. "There's a cut back we can ride through."

Sleeper nodded grimly. "Come on, Bones!" He led, with the stallion. They entered the narrow jaws of the cut-back, and the horses began to struggle up the steep of the slope.

"When we get out, we'll be able to see something around us," said Sleeper, "but now we're in the wolf's throat."

"Got a nice kind of a way of putting things," remarked the girl. "The Colonel took the other valley and came south to warn you! Get the spurs into that fuzztail, Bones. You always rode horses that were only crow-bait."

They began to rise out of the cutback, now they came up among the big boulders at the head of the little valley into sudden view of half a dozen men with leveled guns.

There was nothing to be done. Even Bones, to whom the moment meant the most, did not reach for a weapon; and of course the hands of Sleeper were empty. It was only the girl who snatched out a .45 and said, with a wild flash of her blue eyes: "Shall we try 'em, Bones?"

"Back up, honey," answered Bones. "This game is over and they're raking in table stakes."

Sleeper saw big Bill Collins, the sheriff, stand up from behind a small boulder and come slowly forward, stepping softly to keep his gun from being jarred out of line.

"Stick 'em up, Bones," he said. "I'll be damned if I ever thought that I could turn you into such easy money."

Bones raised his arms straight into the air and held them rigid there. "Sure it's easy money," he said. "Kind of tastes like blood, though, doesn't it?"

There was a perfectly simple explanation. From the high verge of the ravine, Sheriff Bill Collins and his men from White Water had seen the riders in the valley beneath, and when the three bolted suddenly for the cutback, it was easy for the possemen to interpose.

"Kind of a small world!" was the way the sheriff put it. It meant five thousand dollars in head money to him, and a thousand apiece for each of his men.

"What about Sleeper? What does he do in this game?" asked one of the men.

"I dunno," said the sheriff. "I've always aimed to guess that he'd be in trouble, one of these days. A saddle-bum that never does a lick of work is sure to get into bad company sooner or later. Here he is with Bones. Who's the gal, Bones?"

"Ask her."

"What's your name?" asked the sheriff.

Her lip curled as she watched the broad, heavy face of Collins. "Sally Smith is my name," she said.

"Where d'you come from?"

"From Smith County."

"Smith County? Where's that?"

"Over yonder," she said, waving towards half the horizon.

"She's hoorawing you, Bill," said one of the men.

"It looked like to me," said the sheriff, as his men bound Bones' hands behind his back, "that you was pullin' out a gun and aiming to make trouble, Miss Sally Smith."

"How did I know who you were?" asked the girl. "I didn't see your badge. I only saw your mug, and I thought you and the rest were a lot of rustlers."

"Rustlers?" shouted the indignant sheriff.

"Rustlers don't have time to wash, either," she answered, and reined her horse away.

"Bones, I'll be thinking about you," said Sleeper. He rose up on the stallion, holding out his hand.

"Keep back!" snorted Collins.

"Can't I say goodbye to a friend?" asked Sleeper.

"None of your damned monkeyshines, or I'll have you in jail alongside of him. Get your horses, boys. This is a damned lucky day; I told you we'd get our meat."

They started off, and Sleeper watched them go, his head fallen. Gradually the hoofs sounded far and faint.

"And what'll *you* do?" asked the girl.

"Find myself some grub," said Sleeper.

"Yeah. You look that kind," she answered, savagely. "I thought that Bones was a friend of yours."

"He is."

"Ever do you a good turn?"

"Pulled me and the horse out of the creek, when we were drowning. That's all."

She looked curiously at him. "What are you, Sleeper?" she asked.

"A jail-breaker, I guess," he answered, gloomily. "Know anything about that business?"

She stared at him. "You mean for Bones?" she asked.

"Maybe. What are you, sister?"

"Oh, I just sashay around here and there," she answered. "But Bones has to be pulled out of jail."

"You know anything about McGregor and Loftus?"

61

"A pair of old double-crossing snakes. Tinhorns. Four-flushers. Killers. Why Bones ever threw in with them has me beat. The Colonel would have given him a hand when he wanted it."

"Bones was through with that breed," he said.

"That all you can say about the Colonel?"

"I never heard of him before; but he's a sort of a coyote, isn't he?"

"If you could ever get built up to the size of a real man," said the girl, fiercely, "the Colonel would cut you down to a new size and then tell you something about himself."

"Well, so long," said Sleeper.

"You going?"

"You make me sort of tired," said Sleeper. "You've been around some tough hombres, and they've built you up a lot."

"They've what?"

"They've listened to your chatter. It's a funny thing, and a sad thing, too, what listening to a woman will do to her."

"You wouldn't listen to a woman, would you?"

"Only in spots," he said.

"What spots?"

"Supper time, and other eating spots," said Sleeper.

"I'd like to do something about you, brother," said the girl.

"Get your men together and send them to call, some day," he told her. "So long."

"I hate to waste time on you," said Maisry. "But I'd like to know one thing: You really aim to try to help Bones?"

"I'm going to get him out of the jail, if that's what you mean. Or away from the rope, to put it straighter."

Suddenly, the scornful fire died out of her eyes. "I kind of half believe that you're not talking all the way through your hat," she confessed. "Suppose that we go and see the Colonel. He'll want to help."

"Suppose we do," said Sleeper.

11

They found the Colonel after dark, at a little shack not far from White Water. Maisry, as the dimly lighted window of the cabin shone through the brush, whistled twice on a high, sharp note; then she led the way to the door of the house. When she knocked, it was suddenly opened, though no one appeared in the lighted rectangle.

"Well?" demanded a shrill voice that might have belonged to either a child, a man, or a woman.

"I'm here with a hombre I've picked up," said the girl. "Shall we come in?"

"Come in, Maisry," said the high, piping voice, "but I wish you'd stop usin' the whole countryside for a grab-bag. What you brought home this time?"

"Kind of a smart young hombre with a sassy way of talking," said the girl. "Come on in, Sleeper."

She led the way through the door and as Sleeper stepped after her, he found himself in a typical shanty, a sort of wooden tent rather than a house. What was left of a stove, painted red with rust, stood in a corner, propped elaborately from beneath. There was no table. The floor was packed earth. And the chief furnishings were a lantern, a roll of blankets on a tumble-down bunk, and the trappings and saddle of a horse which hung from a peg on the wall. This was a dull background for one of the strangest men that Sleeper had ever seen.

Sleeper thought first of a sack of stilts, or a blue crane with a human face on top of its bunchy body—the Colonel was like that. His legs were too long. They did not leave stomach-room but seemed to divide the man to the chest. His arms and shoulders were extremely long and thick, and his huge head was put down with nothing to speak of in the way of a neck. He had a broad, pale, soggy face, with drooping moustaches and old-fashioned side whiskers which dripped away on either side. His jowls were fat, bluish pouches which set off the paleness of his eyes. He had the look, altogether, of a brooding beast which is digesting and meditating.

"Hello, Sleeper," he said in his high-pitched voice. "Why did you let Maisry get her hands on you? She'll pick you as clean as a bone and throw you over her shoulder."

"Are you making me out a thief?" asked Maisry, carelessly.

"You steal better things than hard cash," answered the Colonel. "Sit down, everybody. There's a stool; and that chair might hold you, Maisry."

"I'm not staying long. You know that Bones is in jail?"

"I know it. He's nearly had his neck stretched, already. The crowd started gathering and yapping. They meant business. It's a long time since they've had the fun of lynchin' anybody in White Water. They sure would of opened that jail and taken out Bones to hang him, but somebody got up and made them a speech and said that it was a shame to hang Bones before he'd had a chance to confess and name all his crimes and his crooked friends. That speech made the crowd hold off for a while."

"Did the fellow who made the speech have long legs and a set of damn silly sideburns?" asked the girl.

The Colonel smiled faintly at her. "Maybe he did. I

wasn't looking him in the face," he said. "What's all this about?"

"Sleeper says that Bones pulled him and his horse out of the water, and now he's going to do something to set Bones free."

The Colonel shook his head. "We may get Bones off with life instead of a rope, but that's the best," he said. "They're going to move Bones from the jail tomorrow—"

"Why not catch him on the road, then?"

"Because he'll have a half dozen men with him, the same men who haven't collected their rewards, yet. And they'll watch him the way a bunch of lobos watch a bogged-down doggie."

"Half a dozen can be rushed!" exclaimed the girl.

"They can," agreed the Colonel, "and ten men can be lost fighting to save one. Does that make any sense?" He snapped his long fingers. "Bones is gone!" he declared. "They're going to take him straight across country to the place where a lot of fools are hankering to hang him."

"I'm sorry," said the girl, with a sigh. "I've always liked Bones. Is he a goner, sure?"

"A dead goner."

"We've got some news, anyway," said the girl to Sleeper. "There's no use bothering about Bones any more."

"No?" said Sleeper. "But I *have* to bother. So long. I'll get started."

"For what? Wait a minute, kid," said the Colonel. "You can't do anything about Bones! I've told you that."

"I've got to appeal the case to a higher authority," said Sleeper. With a wave of the hand he was gone into the night.

Back through White Water Sleeper traced that higher authority. He heard of his man at the saloon. On Careless he followed the trail out of White Water to a shack as wrecked as that in which the Colonel was housed, but found this one unoccupied. He rode on to a farmhouse that stood close to the trail and heard the shouting and laughing of children that burst from the building with more brilliance than the lamplight.

When he heard this, Sleeper smiled and rode closer, until he could see, through the windows of the dining-room, a group of grown people and half a dozen children watching a tall man with a bald head and a bunch on his back taking articles out of a great canvas bag. Already he had scattered queer little toys and dolls over the table, and now, as he went on showing to the house-wife pieces of blue and white patterned cloth he continued a chatter which kept the children whooping with laughter. The wife, however, seemed to be exclaiming over the cheap prices of the peddler.

For a fellow who seemed to distribute so much plea-sure, he had one of the ugliest faces in the world, a very long and downward face with a huge slit of a mouth and a perfectly bald head made him seem old. In fact he could not have been more than in early middle-age. And now and then, in the very midst of his tales and his jesting, he would dart a glance at the rancher or his wife, or even at one of the children, that was like the look of a hawk when it sees prey beneath.

At the hitching rack, Sleeper found three mules that carried packs, their heads hanging patiently as they waited to be relieved from their burdens. When he spotted these poor freighters, Sleeper dismounted from the stal-lion and waited, hunkering on his heels in the shadows.

He did not have to stay there long. The door of the house opened, the peddler appeared with his sack on his back, the door letting out a gust of voices after him. The closing of the door shut out all light and the ped-dler's footsteps came closer to where Sleeper crouched near the hitching rack. There the man opened one of the panniers that hung at the sides of a mule and put his bag inside it, muttering. Sleeper remained motionless.

This muttering of the peddler broke off suddenly. His voice came in a low jarring note: "Who's there?"

At last he had seen the dim outline of the horse against the bushes.

"Hello, Pop," answered Sleeper.

"Sleeper, eh?" exclaimed Pop Lowry. "You never was up this late at night except for deviltry. What you up to now, eh?"

"Looking for a man," said Sleeper.

"What kinda man, eh?"

"A gent who rides mules around the mountains selling stuff for less than he paid for it. A gent who keeps in touch with high-graders bad as himself and uses them on jobs that he plans. A gent who's at the bottom of more trouble than all the rest of the cow-thieves and bandits inside a thousand miles from White Water."

"I dunno who you mean, Sleeper."

"Sure you don't know. It would pain you a lot if you did."

"We're too close to the house," said Pop Lowry. "Let's get out on the road. Then we can talk."

He walked down the lane with the mules trudging after him and Sleeper again on the back of the stallion. When they were in the road, Pop Lowry asked: "What's brought you to me, Sleeper? More trouble, I bet."

"Sure, it's trouble."

"I knew it," said Pop Lowry. "It's a kind of a sad thing the way that people bring their troubles to old Pop Lowry."

"You damn old hypcrite!" exclaimed Sleeper.

"Steady, kid. Don't damn a man that you're going to try to use. You're raisin' my price when you talk like that."

"How d'you know that I'm wanting to use you?"

"I've got a sort of a chill up the middle of the spine and I always know what that means."

"Pop, a fellow called Bones is in the jail. He's a friend of mine."

"They'll hang him sure," the peddler clucked softly. "A fine, high-spirited young fool like you will want to help him out of his troubles. But you can't, Sleeper. I ain't one of those that look down on you. I've had a chance to guess at the stuff that's in you, even if you don't work with your hands. But you can't help Bones. He's a goner, sure!"

"Maybe I can't help him, but *you* can."

"Me? A poor old man like me? You got some funny notions about me, Sleeper! You seem to think that—"

"Can't we talk in the open?" asked Sleeper. "I know what you are, Pop. I'm the only man in this part of the world that even guesses. But in spite of what I know, I've held my tongue, haven't I?"

"The main reason that I got such a respect for you son, is the way you don't go chattering," declared Pop Lowry.

"Bones. I want him free. And with you helping, it can be done. There's mighty little that you can't manage if you put your mind to it."

The peddler chuckled. "A poor old man like me, hobblin' around the roads, workin' like a dog, winter and summer, what do you think I could do to turn Bones free? They're gonna watch him like wolves till they get their blood-money."

"Talk terms, Pop," said Sleeper.

"There ain't any terms. There's ten thousand on the head of Bones. Well, gimme thirty thousand and I'll try what I can do."

"I haven't that much. I haven't any money at all."

"Why d'you waste my time, then?"

"I'll give you something else that you might turn into money—my time."

68

"*Your* time? My God, Sleeper, you drunk?"

"There are things you want done. I'll do 'em. And you'll help me to get Bones out of the jail. I'll sell myself to do anything you want me to do."

"Hey—hold on! Lemme think about that. You'd sell yourself to me?"

"Just that."

"For life, eh?"

"For three months, say."

"Three months? Thirty thousand dollars is my price for helping Bones—it's a damn mean job—the sort of a job I hate. And so you think your time is worth ten thousand a month, eh? What you think that I could do with you?" snarled the peddler.

"I'm not guessing at that. I don't want to guess. You'll send me to hell and back twice a week, I suppose. But I'll do anything if you manage to help Bones."

"Anything?"

"Yes, I said that."

"I do a job worth thirty thousand. Instead of coin, I take the time of a worthless lazy kid for three months. What sort of a fool d'you think that I am, Sleeper? And besides, how would I know that you'd keep your promise?"

"That wouldn't worry you. You know that I keep my word."

The peddler, after a moment, scratched a match and hollowed his hands to throw the light on Sleeper. He quietly endured the shining of the flame. The two big, grimy hands of Lowry looked like lifeless things, the protesting fingers of a copper statue.

"Well, I'll shake hands on it," said the peddler, suddenly.

And dropping the match, he held out his hand. It was Sleeper's turn to pause; but remembering how the rope of poor Bones had pulled him and Careless from the

69

water that day, he caught the hand of Lowry and shook it with a firm grip.

"They're taking Bones away from the jail tomorrow. You better get busy, Pop."

"Tomorrow? Too fast! Too fast! I got no time!" groaned Lowry.

"Start now," urged Sleeper.

"All right, then. You take the mules. Go back through the woods and camp where you find water."

"How'll you be able to find us later on?"

"I could find you the way a bloodhound follers a trail!" said Lowry. "Because it's blood that I'll be hunting!"

12

Back up the side of the mountain, sheltered by a grove of trees, Sleeper slept out the rest of that night after he had stripped the packs from the mules and the saddle from Careless. He slept into the warmth of the morning before Pop Lowry came striding through the trees, stepping big in his cowhide boots.

Sleeper built a cigarette, lighted it, and folded one arm behind his head. "How's things, Pop?" he asked.

Lowry sat down beside him. "Chuck this damned idea," said Lowry. "You can't get Bones free unless hell is raised."

"Raise it, then."

"I tell you, it's a mean job, Sleeper."

"Be mean, then, Pop. Bones has got to be saved."

"You ain't reasonable," said Lowry, "but if you *was*

reasonable, you wouldn't be worth a damn to me!"

He added, after a moment: "I'll stop the bunch who will ride with Bones at a place I'll tell you about. And I'll give you the keys to the irons on his hands and feet. Is that worth three months of your time?"

"How many helpers do you give me?" asked Sleeper.

"Not a one. A crowd can't do the trick. One gent might wangle it, if he's slippery like you are. All a crowd could do would be to make a noise and kill off the bunch of guards. For killing them off I'd want more than three months of your time, Sleeper. I'd want more than all your time, maybe."

Sleeper considered. "All you do is to stop the people who've got Bones with them. And you give me the key to his irons. That's not so much, Pop. No friends at all for me to work with?"

"One man who won't see you if you sneak up on them."

"One man who'll keep his eyes closed, eh?"

"Yes," said Pop. "Little fellow with long hair."

Sleeper, drawing out the long hunting knife, began to play with it, as was his habit when his mind was occupied. Pop Lowry, fascinated, watched the knife wheel in the air and descend, always caught by the deadly point on the ball of Sleeper's thumb. It was like seeing a snake caught by the fangs as it lunged.

He kept lifting his glance from the flash of the knife to Sleeper's brooding eyes. Finally he said: "You're a queer one, Sleeper. I'd rather have poison poured into my coffee than you on my trail."

Sleeper said nothing. At last, slipping the knife away, he remarked: "It's the best that I can do. What's the look of the man who'll close his eyes if I come up?"

"You make the bargain?"

"I make the bargain. Three months of my time against this."

The eyes of the peddler flashed and he held out his

71

hand. "Shake on it, kid, and then I'll talk," he said.

"Wash your hand before you offer it to me," said Sleeper evenly. "I've given you my word, and that's enough."

The peddler looked curiously down at his hand and then up at Sleeper's cold face. "You hate me a good deal, kid, don't you?" he asked.

"More than anything else I know," answered Sleeper.

"Kind of a funny damn thing that we gotta throw in together, ain't it?" asked Pop Lowry.

"Call it that," said Sleeper. "Slip me the keys and tell me where I'm to expect the guards."

"Here," said Lowry.

He took out a flat-headed key and passed it over. "The same key fits the leg shackles and the handcuffs. And the place you'll find them will be over on the Thomas Flats. You know where the old draw runs across the Thomas Trail?"

"I know. There's a ravine down there with a lot of scrub growing in the bottom."

"That's it. It makes a pretty good camping place, with some water that's good enough for cattle and does for humans, too. That's where they'll stop tonight."

Sleeper's eyes narrowed thoughtfully. "How can you put on the brakes to stop them just there?"

"A couple of horses are gonna go lame, it appears," said Pop Lowry. He grinned, and his long, yellow teeth flashed like the teeth of a dog.

Sleeper nodded. "All right. Run along and let me sleep, then."

Lowry stood up, stretched himself, and looked down with interest at Sleeper. "If they don't get your scalp," he said, "I'm gonna use you to whittle out a lot of funny shapes of things. So long, kid. I'm glad that Bones has a friend, and I'm glad that the friend needed old Pop." He laughed, waved a hand, and went off to repack the mules.

Afterwards, from the misty distance of sleep, the voice cut into Sleeper's drowsing. "I'll be out at the old shack. You know where—near White Water. You report there if you get Bones loose from trouble. So long, kid."

He was gone. One of the mules brayed far away; and as this trumpet died out, silence fell around Sleeper. The copper-bright stallion commenced to graze closer to him, lifting his head now and then to mark a change of scents on the wind, or a stir of shadows beneath the trees. . . .

It was already deep afternoon when he looked at the sun to gauge the time, washed at the water hole, dressed, and mounted the stallion. Sleep had rubbed a soothing hand right across the brow of care. He was ready for anything, now, and he began to sing as he took the way down the slope and through the town of White Water.

A girl on a swift-moving gray mare rounded a corner and galloped past him, the sun bright in her hair. As she saw Sleeper, she pulled her mare around and came up beside him. The horse had cost money; so had the girl. Her tan riding clothes had a special softness of texture that was like a dollar sign to the eye, and the silver on her hand-tooled bridle was the finest Mexican work, delicate beyond thought.

"Hey, Sleeper!" she called.

"Hey, Kate," said he, and pulled off his battered hat.

Her eyes were shining. He took a fresh pleasure in finding them brown. From a distance, she looked like one of those blue and golden beauties; the quiet brown of her eyes was always a surprise.

"Sleeper," she said, "you haven't been near me for days. Why don't you drift out to the house now and then?"

"I'm a little afraid of your father, Kate."

"Why, Sleeper, he says that you're one of the great people, really. You don't have to be afraid of him any longer."

"All right. I'll try not to be."

"What's become of all your money? You're in rags again."

"You see, I ran into a faro game and felt lucky. But I was wrong."

"You'll be betting the hide of Careless, one of these days."

He sleeked the neck of the great horse, and Careless turned his head with a softening eye. "No, I won't bet Careless," he said quietly.

"But Sleeper, when are you going to grow up?"

There was a good deal of meaning behind that inquiry. He looked down at the sun-brightened dust and saw the shadows of the legs of the horses stenciled in black across it.

"I'm trying hard to get older," he answered. "Maybe time will help me."

"You ought to start work—steady work, Sleeper!" she insisted. "Father will give you a place. Not just daubing ropes on cattle, but something with a future in it."

"Would he?" repeated Sleeper. His eye grew clear and bright. "I'm going to do it, one day," he answered. "I've got my hands full for a month or two, just now. And after that—I'm going to turn over a new leaf."

"Do you mean it, Sleeper?"

"I do mean it," he said grimly.

"Old Sleeper!" said the girl, half sadly, half smiling. "You always have the right intentions but they don't grow very fast, do they? Where are you bound for now?"

"Oh, I'm bound out."

"It's always the out-trail for you," sighed the girl. "Give me your hand, Sleeper."

He gave her his hand. She stripped off her riding glove before she took it, like a man.

"You'll come home and remember me, Sleeper?" she said.

"Remember you? There's never a minute that I'm not thinking of you!" he exclaimed.

"Goodbye, my dear," said the girl.

She turned her horse back down the street, and he rode the stallion from White Water into the open. Great resolutions were sweeping up into his mind as mountains sweep upon the eye.

There was no one else like Kate Williams, with the delicacy of a woman and the courage of a man. As soon as he had finished this business and the work of Pop Lowry, he would come back to her. He *would* settle down. He *would* get a job. And even when the days seemed endless and the course of the year one long agony, he would cling to his duty. That sort of thing, he ruminated, must be the common fate of man. And if a fellow tries to escape it, his life is ruined, together with all the lives of the people around him. But he, Sleeper, no longer would waste his life, whittling in the sun.

He would show people that he was capable of continued effort. He might go to the legislature or something, in the end. He would be called an example for youth. And in the meantime, he would marry Kate Williams. Never take a penny of her father's money, but live in a hardworking poverty; honorable and industrious, a clean, meager, hard life. . . .

He had reached such a point in his reflections that his breath was coming shorter and his breast heaving higher, and there was a thin moisture of self-pity and desperate resolve in his eyes, also. But at this moment, a shadow moved through the brush at his right, and out flashed a lively pinto mustang ridden by Maisry. She waved her hand and called to him as she came up.

"Hello, Sleeper. Want some company?" she demanded.

Seen from a distance, she looked like a beautiful Indian girl. Seen at close hand, the blue of her eyes was a shock of surprise and delight. He saw her, now, at close hand; and he felt the fullness of that shock.

"Company to where?" he asked.

"To Thomas Flats," she answered.

"Who've you been talking to?" he demanded.

"You know. Old Pop Lowry. He seemed to have some ideas." She winked and then laughed.

"What's your last name, Maisry?" he asked.

"Maisry Fellows is what I'm called."

"Maisry Fellows, will you do something for me?"

"That's why I'm here," she replied.

"Then go home and stay there."

She frowned at him. "What home?" she asked.

"Any home. But start moving, will you?"

"Don't be so big and mean," answered the girl. "You know what you're up against, and an extra pair of hands may do you a lot of good."

He stared at her. When she was angry, a glow came over over her. "What's a big tramp like Bones mean to you?"

"He taught me how to shoot."

"You're good, are you?"

"This good," she said.

A thin shadow trailed over them. As the girl lifted her head, Sleeper looked up and saw the hawk swinging low towards the ground, turning its pointed, evil head from side to side. The next moment a gun barked and the hawk toppled from its place as though from the edge of an invisible cliff. It hit the ground hard not twenty feet away.

"That's pretty goot shooting—with a pop-gun," he remarked, noting her .32.

"Let me have your .45, then, and I'll show you!" she declared.

"I haven't got a gun."

"You haven't—what?"

"I haven't a gun."

"Wait a minute. I thought you were going to—"

"I don't use guns. They weigh too much," explained Sleeper. She stared in her turn, struck pale with astonishment. "You mean that you're going to tackle—"

"You run along home and stop asking questions. Pop had no business talking to you, anyway."

"Sleeper, are you clean loco? They'll eat you, alive!"

"This comes of Pop talking to females!" he growled.

"Pop Lowry knew that you needed somebody along to take care of you," said the girl. "And I'm going every inch of the way!"

13

Dusk poured the draw full of a blue silvery haze, still there was some light from the horizon over the flats, but in the draw the fire of the camp gleamed like a searching eye. They were down under the high edge of the draw as he said to the girl: "You stay here and keep the horses for me."

"We'll tie the horses. I'm going on with you."

"You take my orders and obey them!"

He could feel rather than see the anger in her eyes. "I'd like to hit you, Sleeper!" she said through her teeth.

"My God, you're pretty!" exclaimed Sleeper, illogically, and he took her in his arms and kissed her.

Where was the ghost of Kate Williams then?

"Let me go!" said the girl. "Except for making a racket

and giving the show away, I'd make some trouble for this, you sneaking coyote!"

"You're beautiful!" said Sleeper, and kissed her again. Then he stepped back from her. "I'm sorry," he said.

"Do I go on with you now?" she pleaded, quite overlooking his actions.

"You stay back here with the horses."

She groaned but did not argue, so he left her and commenced stalking the camp. What had Lowry meant by talking? Above all, what had he meant by talking to a girl?

He came through the lower fringe of trees. Between him and the campfire was the level surface of the water hole. The flame painted it with long orange streamers, dazzling bright except when one of the moving shadows near to the fire walked across its light and killed the reflection. There were seven men in that camp and one of them was Bones, of course. At a little distance from the men, the horses were hobbled to graze on the tall, rich grass. In the shaking of the fire light, they looked like nameless monsters.

Sleeper slipped back inside the brush and moved around the expanse of the water until the firelight shone strongly at him through the leaves. Then he went forward on hands and knees. He could hear the voices inside the camp clearly.

Sheriff Bill Collins was posting a guard which was to walk up and down in the brush or along the edge of it.

His speech was of interest.

"We got a ten thousand dollar package of goods along with us. A thing that's worth the stealing. If he's worth ten thousand to the law, he's worth a pile more to his friend, maybe. We've got to keep our eyes open. Three of us walk guard for three hours. Then the next three for the next three hours. And after that, we'll make our start. Understand? You boys step out there and keep your eyes open. Look mighty sharp. If you see anything stir, shoot first and holler second."

The guard was instantly posted. As they began to walk up and down, Sleeper shrank flat in a patch of tall grass fenced on either side by small shrubs. The path of one of the guards passed within three steps of him and he had to make himself small.

He could see that there was little chance to withdraw, and no chance at all of making an approach closer to the fire until the guards were changed. That meant three hours of lying on the cold, damp ground. If he fell asleep, he might snore; so he'd have to stay awake.

By a great effort of will he worked the nervous tremors out of his arms and legs and lay very still. The cold from the ground seemed to soak up through him as though his body were porous.

And so the time wore by like a snail, hour after hour of the monotonous silence.

There was little talk at the campfire. Tall Bones sat up, making a slight jingling of his chains whenever he moved. Once Collins said: "How does it feel to be worth ten thousand bucks, Bones?"

And Bones answered: "Ask me how it feels to be dead, will you? I ain't gonna see any of the money I'm sold for!" After that, Bones lay down and the sheriff followed.

The little man with the long hair was not by the fire. He was the one of the three guards who moved up and down on the farther side of the camp and now and then it was he who came in and put fresh fuel on the flames. As he did this, on two occasions he stood up and looked earnestly around him. That attitude of his had a definite meaning for Sleeper. The man was expecting something.

Something rustled in the grass behind Sleeper. He started as beside him a body slid to rest and the whisper of Maisry Fellows said: "I couldn't wait it out any longer, Sleeper. Sorry!"

"You three-ply idiot!" murmured Sleeper in answer. "Back out of this!"

"I can't without being noticed!" whispered the girl. "Look at that damn moon coming up to spoil everything!"

It appeared as a flaming pyramid in the east, a pyramid that brightened by degrees and waxed, until the wide, yellow rim of the moon appeared. It increased, clung for a moment by the lower rim, like a bubble stuck to a glass edge. Then it was detached and floated softly up the sky, shrinking a little, growing less yellow, casting every moment a brighter and a whiter light.

No sun, it seemed to Sleeper, ever had shone with such deadly force. The flat of the bottomland was streaked with intense shadows overlaid upon clear silver. And how could the eyes of the guards fail to find two figures that lay only half hidden behind the brush and in the grass?

"It's great, isn't it?" whispered the girl.

"Grand," said Sleeper sourly. "Helpful as hell to us, right now."

"Are you afraid?"

"Yeah—plenty. How about you?"

"Frightened silly—and I love it!"

He grinned a little as he heard this. It had the true, honest tang to it. That other figure, that brown-eyed Kate, became rather dim in his mind. Black hair and blue eyes—that seemed the only proper color with which beauty should be stained.

The guard in front of him suddenly walked up to the fire and said. "Turn out, you fellows! Turn out! Our three hours are up!"

Sleeper was out of his place in the grass in an instant, gliding forward. He had spotted a patch of brush well inside the circle around which the guards marched. It was daring danger to make this move, but at least he would be within reaching distance of the prisoner from here.

And as he sank into the shubbery, he felt a sudden relief, having taken a step from which there was no drawing back. But at the same moment, striking him as unexpectedly as a blow on the back, a sneeze exploded from his throat.

"What's that?" shouted the voice of Bill Collins. "There in that bush!"

And Sleeper had no gun. He had only his knife, and the cold handle of that was instantly in the grasp of his fingers when he heard the voice of the girl say, from behind him: "Well, does it throw a chill into all you gents to hear a girl sneeze?"

She was walking calmly into the camp, covering up his telltale exploit with her presence.

"What's that?" two or three shouted. "It's the girl— it's Maisry," said the sheriff. "What the devil are you doing here, Maisry Fellows? What are you up to?"

"Maisry, have you gone loco?" demanded the husky voice of Bones.

"I wanted to see you again, Bones," said the girl. "How are things?"

"Pretty fair. You're crazy to come down here this time of night."

"Just a lot of big brothers, all these hombres," said the girl. "And I like to travel in the cool of the night. Why not?"

"I thought that sneeze sounded nearer. I thought it sounded right out of that brush, there," insisted Bill Collins.

"I'll take a look," answered a voice. It was the little man with the long hair. He walked straight into the patch of shrubbery—and struck his foot against the body of the hidden man.

Sleeper, his arms drawn back with the knife, waited.

He saw the convulsive start of the other, then he heard the little man of the long hair saying, calmly enough: "Why, I dunno what you heard, but it sure didn't come from here, unless this scrub oak an' blackjack can sneeze by itself."

"Is there anything I can do for you?" asked the girl of Bones. "I didn't have a chance to talk to you before they slammed you into the jail. You tell me what you want, and maybe I can get it for you, and send it along. You still have friends in the world. Don't you forget that, Bones."

"Thanks," said Bones. "I'll tell you what you can do for me, sister. Hike out of here, and hike fast."

"Where's your hoss?" asked the suspicious sheriff.

"Over there. I left him back there while I made sure that this was really the camp that I was hunting for."

"Hoping you might sneak up and give Bones a hand, eh?" sneered Bill Collins. "Wouldn't it of been sweet if a smoothfaced brat like you had took Bones away from six growed-up men? I dunno why you done this, kid, but now git out of here and git fast. We don't wanta be bothered."

"Thanks, Sheriff," said the girl. "And so-long, Bones. Sorry about everything."

She walked away from the fire, slowly, and straight past the undergrowth where Sleeper lay. Passing it, her step slowed until it seemed that she was about to halt, but she mastered that impulse and went straight on into the taller shrubbery. The crackling of the branches ceased. She was gone.

In the meantime, the second guard had taken its post, with the sheriff among its members.

"The jails is too full of men," was his comment on this visit. "There had oughta be a little room left for the girls—sassy brats like that one." And he began to walk his beat, just behind the waiting form of Sleeper.

The relieved guards, well tired by their duties, were

82

quickly wrapped up and asleep, all except the little man with the long hair. He, on the contrary, seemed to have something in mind which kept him wide awake. It was thought for his horse, perhaps. For now he stood up and brought from the hobbled line of grazing animals a good, upstanding gelding, from the legs of which he took the sideline and the hobbles. He pulled a bridle over its head.

"What's the idea there?" demanded the sheriff.

"I'm kind of worried," said the little man. "Suppose something was to happen—suppose a gent instead of a girl showed up—well, there's not a hoss in the camp that's ready to be moved."

"That's good sense, too," said Collins. "That's more sense than you ever showed before, Pete."

He resumed his beat, while Pete turned and sat again by the fire, near the prone figure of Bones.

And right up into the shadow cast by Pete moved the flat, slithering body of Sleeper. He entered that long, slanting shadow from the fire, but still the moon shone on him with plenty of light. He could only hope that he might not be seen by any of the guards for the simple reason that they would not look for him there.

Now he was reaching to Bones, whispering: "Bones, it's Sleeper. Lie still. Don't stir. I've got the key!"

And the faint whisper of Bones answered: "You damn young fool, them buzzards will pick you clean an' leave your bones rotting here!"

He found the handcuffs, scratched softly with the point of the key until he located the entrance slot, and in another moment Bones' wrists were free. He took the key in his own fingers and sat up.

"What's the matter, there?" called the voice of the sheriff.

"I'm gonna smoke," answered Bones, and at the same time worked the key into his ankle irons.

Ahead of them, a low, guarded voice said: "Pretend

to hit me over the head and knock me out. I'm leavin' my gun lyin' on the ground—"

"The horse is right behind you, Bones," whispered Sleeper. "Grab it and jump on its back. Head straight across the bottom to the south. Straight across. I've got my horse there."

Bones nodded silently. "I'd like to salt away some of these gizzards with lead," he whispered a moment later.

There was a very soft clicking sound which told that his feet were free also. "Now!" said Sleeper. "On the run, Bones!"

For his own part, he whirled to his feet as Bones arose. The sheriff, behind him, cursed and cried out: "Stop! Who's there?"

Sleeper struck Pete's head with the flat of his hand and Pete keeled over as though he had been hit by a sledgehammer.

Bones' long, lanky body leaped for the horse.

"Wake up! Turn out! Hell's loose!" yelled the sheriff, and fired. He put one bullet somewhere through space. Then a streak of light left the right hand of Sleeper. He threw the knife from the flat of his palm, whipping it across the tips of his fingers. It was a simple thing to do if one was born for it and had had twenty years' constant practice. The knife was not aimed at the breast of the sheriff, or he would have been a dead man on the spot. It was directed towards his right shoulder, and through the flesh of that shoulder it glided.

The lawman dropped his rifle with a yell and caught out the weapon that was buried in his flesh. Past him flashed the racing mustang with Bones riding bareback on it. Past him went the streaking form of Sleeper.

"Sleeper! It's that damn kid—it's Sleeper—oh, damn your heart, you've ruined me!" shouted the sheriff. "Horses! Horses! For God's sake get the horses! We've let ten thousand dollars slip through our fingers, you fools!"

Sleeper, hearing the voice, listened to the crackling of gunfire, heard the bullets rush through the branches about him.

He had been recognized, and he knew what that meant—a life of stealth outside the law—a life of cold wandering, cast from the law-abiding society of men.

He was an outlaw from this moment. And that word had always brought up into his mind the picture of a lone wolf, skulking, head down, through the white rage of a blizzard, hunching its gaunt belly against its backbone.

He had that picture and went blind with it. A moment later he slipped, struck against a tree, and fell back on the ground with his breath thoroughly knocked out of him. His brain was clear enough. It told him to get at once on his feet, and that he could not be defeated by such a silly chance at this time. He did in fact regain his feet, but he was doubled over, gasping, and his legs staggered, weak at the knees, when he tried to run. Like a man shot through the belly he struggled forward, biting at the air with his teeth, like that very picture of the wolf which he had conceived.

And behind him, the sound of galloping horses had begun!

He gasped for breath. He could never get to the place where the girl had tethered the horses. They would sweep up on him and shoot him down—

Instead, he stood still, drew in a desperate breath, and whistled a sharp, shrill note. Then he staggered forward again. Every muscle in his bruised chest and stomach was tensed, hard as a board. And other hoofbeats swept towards him; he knew the long sweep and rhythm of them. Careless had heard the call and had broken away. He would have snapped strong ropes to answer that whistle!

Here he came, as Sleeper shouted with a gasping breath. The moonlight turned the beautiful horse to silver, to flowing, wet silver. He was beside his master. He was ready at hand, as Sleeper pulled himself up into the saddle. There were no reins for him to grasp. They had been broken off close to the bit, but reins were hardly needed. A pressure of the knees or of the hand would guide Careless when his master was mounted on him.

The hard rushing of the hoofs, the shouting behind threatened like a wave to overwhelm them, but in another moment the stallion was off. And he left the confusion and the danger behind him as a rising bird leaves the ground.

Through the last of the brush he galloped. The unbroken sweep of prairie showed, and the steep bank of the draw. He went up it like a springing goat up a mountainside. And on the level above appeared the girl and Bones—she with her rifle drawn from the saddle boot, ready to cover the retreat.

There was no need for rifle-fire, now. There was only need to follow the headlong pace of the stallion, if they could. And behind them, from the draw, came a wild outburst of yelling. It sounded to Sleeper like the baying of hounds.

The chase lasted only a short time. In the next draw they doubled back out of sight and sound of the man-hunt. Before dawn they were in the high hills where they made a pause and looked out over the plain, still dark with the lower shades of night.

They had loosened the cinches of the horses. They stood on either side of the girl with their arms interlocked behind her. And she looked up to one face and then to the other in a fervor of enthusiasm.

"It was the greatest night of my life!" she cried. "It was better than dancing with the King of England. It was wonderful, Bones; it was glorious, Sleeper! And what a man you turned out to be!"

He smiled, not at the girl but at the darkness of the

wide world before him. That was how life seemed to him, and all the future, filled with danger.

Bones reached a hand across to him and he gripped it silently. Sleeper then had a strange and perfect sense of duty fulfilled. He had embarked upon the out-trail where he had to go, and it made no difference if the trail never turned back.

14

Sleeper stood very still for a second, on the deep creek bank. In the meadow across the stream ran the golden stallion, Careless, racing with its head thrown high, canting toward its master. . . . but now, both man and horse had ceased their play and each stood statue still, listening, intent.

Sleeper turned, studying the brushes off to the left alertly. Then he shrugged, a slight puzzled frown appearing on his tanned forehead beneath the brim of his battered hat.

He jerked his hand toward his head and the chestnut came at full speed with his mane fluttering high and tail stretched straight by the speed of the gallop.

From lip to lip, the creek was twenty-five or thirty feet across but the stallion made nothing of it. He shot high into the air, struck well in on the farther bank, and then rounded breathing deeply to the side of his master.

Sleeper took a few pieces of sugar from his pocket and fed them to the big stallion, one by one. Even that he should be able to offer his horse a treat as cheap as this seemed surprising, considering the ragged clothes in which he was dressed. The only things new were the good moccasins on his feet, true Indian work decorated with a bright patterning of beads. His hair was black, his skin was almost dark enough to give him the look of Indian blood, but the blue of his eyes told a different story.

The stallion whirled about and threw up its head. It made no sound but its whole attitude was one of challenge. Sleeper, with a subtle gesture, brought a knife into the flat of his hand. It was perfectly concealed, the handle remaining up his sleeve, but a flick of hand and wrist would throw that knife as straight as ever a bullet flew.

Again, from the brush he heard a light crackling noise and presently there came into view a string of three mules, the first pair carrying heavy packs and the third bearing two wicker panniers. At the rear stalked the peddler with long, slow steps. The bunch behind his shoulders looked less like a deformity than a knapsack —he stood straight enough. He carried a walking stick tall enough to be called a staff, and on this he leaned as the mules came into the open.

"Hi, Sleeper!" he called.

"Hi, Pop," said Sleeper.

"I seen you from the hill running Careless. How do you manage that, Sleeper?" Pop Lowry asked.

"A dog can do that—and a horse like Careless can do anything that a dog can manage," said Sleeper.

"Stand up and beg, f'rinstance?" suggested the peddler.

Sleeper made a sweeping gesture—the stallion reared instantly and struck a balance by beating at the air with its forelegs. Another gesture brought him back to all fours, and Sleeper affectionately rubbed the stallion's muzzle.

"Well, doggone my eyes!" said Pop Lowry. "What else have you been teaching him?"

"To catch a rope in his teeth and pull—to slide back the bar of a gate—to kneel down or lie down—to come to a whistle when he can't see me—to go through brush without making a sound—to walk a log like a circus performer; and to fetch my clothes or shoes or anything else I point out. Like this!"

His hand flicked. The knife, like a line of light, left his fingers, shot past the head of the peddler with hardly an inch to spare, and lodged in a narrow sapling, where it stuck humming like an angry wasp.

"Confound you, Sleeper," shouted Pop Lowry. "I thought that steel was aimed for my brain!"

"Go fetch it, boy,' said Sleeper.

The stallion went to the knife, gripped the handle of it, and worked it up and down for an instant to free it from the wood. Then he tugged the knife out and brought it back to his master. Sleeper palmed the knife with a motion of the hand too swift for the eye to follow.

"Always wasting time, eh?" growled Pop Lowry. "Foolin' around with a horse, playin' with a knife like a kid. When are you gonna grow up, Sleeper?"

"When I get through working for you, Pop. But here's two days of my three months used up, and you haven't asked me to do a thing. Couldn't you think of anything hard enough?"

"There's eighty-eight days left. You'll be busy," said Pop.

"Busy or dead," said Sleeper. "What's the first thing you want me to do—since I'm the slave?"

"Kind of a queer job," said Pop Lowry. "You wouldn't guess what it is."

"To get a man in the Diablo Mountains," suggested Sleeper.

The peddler straightened suddenly and his long jaw dropped. Pockmarks made his face hideous at all times, but suspicion made it even more ugly now.

"Who've you been talkin' to?" he asked. "How'd you know that I want you to get a man in the Diablos?"

"You looked south at them in a queer way when I asked what you wanted me to do," Sleeper answered mysteriously. "And what else could I fetch for you from the Diablos? There's nothing but rattlesnakes and men down there."

"You got a funny brain in your head," scowled Pop Lowry. "But it gets results, and those are what count. Yeah—I want you to get me a man in the Diablos—one of Gil Fanwick's outfit."

"How many gunfighters are you going to send along with me?" Sleeper asked.

"Nobody," said Pop Lowry. "Gil is a kind of a friend of mine and I don't want no killing."

"I walk right into a bunch of outlaws and come out with one of them? Is that all?" Sleeper wanted to know. "Fanwick has the meanest crowd of man-killers that ever rode on leather. They chew lead instead of gum."

"It's a job that needs a right cool head and a steady hand, maybe," said Pop. "That's why I come to you, Sleeper!"

"Who's the fellow I have to catch?"

"By name of Stan Douglas—son of Champ Douglas."

"Has he gone wrong?"

"Started that way. Gets into a ruction with his old man because old Champ won't pay a gamblin' debt of the kid. And Stanley pulls up and quits home. He runs away and joins up with Gil Fanwick. And the idea is to get him away and take him home before he rides with Gil on some damn raid. The old man is pretty nigh crazy!"

"He'll pay big for that, Pop."

"I dunno," said Lowry. "Mostly I'm interested in seein' the kid taken home safe and sound."

Sleeper smiled. "What's he paying?" he asked. "Fifty —sixty thousand?"

Pop answered, scowling: "You ain't hired to ask so damn many questions."

"All right," said Sleeper. "How long have I got to make the clean-up for you?"

"About two days," said Lowry. "If the bunch starts anything, you see that the kid don't take a part in it. Understand? Go up to the town of San Miguel. Somewheres near there is where Fanwick's gang hides out. They don't hide much, neither. They own the folks around there because Fanwick believes in payin' for the beef and the horses he uses. He pays double the market price and those hombres down there all swear by him. Which is nacheral and right. Like a wise dog, he don't foul his own kennel, and he leaves his dead men a long ways off. If a posse starts up through the Diablos after Fanwick, every mother's son on that range is out to help the crooks get away."

"That makes my job look easy," said Sleeper. "Everybody in the range against me, and Fanwick's gunmen on top of the rest."

"Why, kid," said Lowry, "you never was cut out for easy jobs. You'd go to sleep, sure, if you was to try your hand at an easy job. I've just picked out a little thing that'll keep you stirred up and on your toes."

"Thanks," said Sleeper. "How's Bones, these days?"

"He's doin' fine. Layin' low and puttin' on flesh. He swears that he'll die for you if you ever as much as lift a finger for him to come. And the poor gent don't know that you sold yourself to me for three months in order to help him out of trouble."

"I don't want him to know," answered Sleeper, "but I could use a fellow like Bones on this kind of a job."

"Numbers won't help you. Brains is all that you can use—and maybe a fast hoss like Careless. But you can't take him with you."

"Why not?"

"A hoss with the looks of Careless? He'd be stole in five minutes by the Fanwick gents."

"I'll have to take my chances," said Sleeper, sourly. "Careless stays with me. He goes off his feed when I'm not around."

"Do it your own way," answered Lowry. "What'll be your first step?"

"I won't know till I get on the spot," answered Sleeper. "So long!"

15

In the town of San Miguel in the Diablo Mountains, the largest building next to the church was the hotel which was run by Carlos Oñate. That is to say, the hotel was owned by him, but it was run by his wife, Rosita—because she was a bigger man than her husband.

It was she who woke on this night, and heard the voice of the gringo calling from the street below: "Hello! Hello! Hey, landlord! I don't want to spend the night in the streets! Let me in, will you?" Then the cry changed to very good Mexican, and the call was repeated.

Rosita hoisted herself upon one elbow and kicked her husband with her knee. He woke hastily, with a grunt, between two snores. "Ah, Rosita!" he said as his eyes were open. He seemed to know that touch.

"Listen, Carlos," she said. "You hear the gringo dog howling in the street? It is true that we are in the United States, but may my blood change to water before I ever take from the gringos anything but money—a curse on the air they breathe! Now we have the hotel full to the last room. There is a good excuse. Go down at once and tell the dog to go and howl at another door. We have no room and we have no wish for him here!"

"That may make bad feeling, if the thing is repeated," said Carlos, nevertheless obediently getting from the bed to his feet, because he had long ago learned that it was best way to begin to obey, even if the cause were worth an argument.

"We have the house full," said Rosita, "and as for bad feeling, that devil of a Gil Fanwick is our friend, at last, and what else do we care?"

"Do you think," said Carlos, hesitantly, "that I could dare to open the door of the patio and go out to him? Do you think that I could dare to kick him down the street?"

"My dear," said the wife, with an unusual tenderness, "I shall go to the window and watch you! Kick him as far as you please, my own Carlos, my sweet!"

Carlos stepped into heavy shoes, pulled on a pair of trousers, and jammed a big sombrero on his head. Even in the middle of the night, he felt undressed unless he had that sombrero over his eyes. In order to clear his eyes and rouse his spirit, he found by sense of smell the string of onions which had been hung across the room to dry. Taking one of these, he began to eat it like an apple as he descended the stairs.

"The fool has a step like a workhorse," said Rosita to herself. "He will rouse all the guests."

But since nearly all of these were Mexicans who would appreciate a good joke at the expense of an *Americano*, she got her bulk out of bed and leaned her full bosom against the casement so that she could peer down into the street.

The moon was not in perfect position to show all the

picture. It glowed on the whitewashed walls of the old dobe church up the street and it showed to Rosita a slender, ragged youth in front of the big patio gate. As for the horse, it was lost, almost, in the shadow nearer the wall, like something deep under water.

Presently, Carlos cleared his throat in the patio and clanked open the great iron bolt of the patio gate. Then Carlos stepped forth. He had grown a little heavy in the belly, of late years, but he was a stout man. His forward-leaning head gave him a bullish appearance.

The *Americano* began pleasantly to ask for quarters. Carlos replied like an angry watch dog. More words passed. The *Americano* seemed to shrink away. Big Carlos, following, launched a kick which was famous all through the Diablo Mountains. And then something strange happened. . . .

Rosita rubbed her eyes. She could not believe what they told her. But it seemed certain that Carlos had been hurled backward through the shadows of the open patio gate!

She held her breath. But as the American took his horse and started to lead it through the gap, there was the sound of the gate being slammed, and the heavy bolt being driven home. There followed the groaning murmur of Carlos from the court. He had been badly hurt, but he managed, like a prudent host, to get to his feet and secure the gate.

Rosita breathed very hard, so that her nostrils flared. Her great hands opened and closed again into fists. She wished that she had been present in person at that scene down the stairs, and she was about to descend to the battle as the voice of the American arose, again speaking quite good Spanish: "Landlord! Landlady! Am I to sleep in the street?"

Then she remembered her three tall sons. Each was taller than his father. Each feared nothing under God,

94

either with knives or at wrestling. So she stepped to the inner door and pulled it open. Three snores, all deep, all resonant, greeted her from the darkness.

"Miguel! Pedro! Juan!" she called.

Three musically intermingling snores answered her. She leaned, found a heavy boot, and threw it at the nearest prostrate, dusky figure. A long and rippling Mexican oath, embracing the names of half a dozen saints, answered her. The figure sprang up.

"Down to the court!" said the mother. "Go down, Miguel. Waken your two brothers, the snoring pigs. An *Americano* is beating the life from your father. Go down and break him into little pieces. I give you permission."

She went back to her window in the front room with a certain balm of expectation already warming her heart; and behind her and beneath her she heard the rumbling of three pairs of feet which were descending to the battle.

When she thought of her three sons, she thought of three great notes on a trumpet—she thought of angels in blue and gold—she thought of three great and strong gods.

She was in time, at her casement, to see the patio gate fling open, and, in a close body, the three strong men issued forth. She heard them snarl, not overloudly, but like dogs each about to take possession of a bone. Almost, in her heart, she pitied the slender, solitary *Americano*. They swooped upon him. They rose over him, like a great stampede of bulls over a tethered calf. They closed upon him.

An obscurity of whirling followed. She could not see very well. A great form, she saw, had hurled grotesquely through the air and descended face down with a mighty flop in the dust of the street. It looked like Miguel, and Miguel did not rise again.

Another bulky figure began to stagger, like an athlete

95

running backwards. It crashed almost head on against the wall beside the gate and then pitched to the side. This form, also, did not rise. The third man, tearing himself clear, turned and fled through the open gate like one with wildcats on his back, and disappeared.

Then the slender *Americano* took his horse and led it out of view into the patio. Rosita Oñate rubbed her eyes twice, took a great breath, and went straightway to the second room which opened off the sleeping quarters which she occupied with her husband. She threw the door open and stepped into an atmosphere flavored with a delicate aroma, as of flowers.

It was the chamber of Anna, her daughter—Anna, tall, graceful, lovely as a single rose in a garden of cactus.

"Anna, child!" murmured the mother.

"Well?" said Anna, sleepily.

"There is a man in the patio," said Rosita.

"Let him stay there," answered Anna.

"Anna," said the mother, "there is a *man* in the patio!"

"Ah!" said Anna, and was instantly out of her bed.

For her, while her mother lighted a lamp with a badly smoked chimney, it was the work of a moment to don a dress, slip her graceful feet into straw *huarches,* thrust a rose into her hair, practice one smile at the dazzled mirror, and then seize the lamp from Rosita's hand.

"Your poor father—and then all your three brothers," said the mother, tenderly. "I fear that they may have broken bones. But it's a long time since we've been certain that there was a man in the house!"

"Only last Sunday," said the girl, "I burned two candles as an offering—and this is my answer, no doubt!"

She descended the stairs while the lamp cast a smoky glory about her dark young head. Then Rosita went back into her room as a groaning figure dragged itself across the threshold. It was the voice of poor Carlos, saying: "My leg is almost broken at the hip. The devil, the *Amer-*

96

icano, turned himself into three men. While I kicked at one, the other two both hit me behind each ear. My skull is fractured. Call for the doctor, in the name of God!"

"I might send for the veterinary," said Rosita, "but only a fool will spend money to mend a pig. There was only one *Americano* but you were only a third of a man. I saw it all."

Rosita now set open the door of her room, opening on the main stairs, and she heard voices rising, and saw the loom of a light that was mounting. The voice of a man sang softly an old Spanish song:

> *The sea was of mountains;*
> *The mountains were thunder;*
> *The way had no ending*
> *When I journey from Anna.*
>
> *The sea was of silk;*
> *The mountains were meadows;*
> *The road was a step*
> *When I came home to Anna.*

Here the song and the noise of steps ended. The knocking at a door broke the brief silence, and a sleepy voice asked what was the matter. The slender stranger offered to wager five dollars against the bed of the guest—and the bet to be decided with the guest's own dice.

"In this," said Rosita, sighing and shaking her head, "the *Americano* proves himself to be a fool." But a little later, still, she heard a sharp, bright exclamation from Anna. And, still later, she heard a voice hissing soft Mexican curses, and a dragging step which passed down the stairs.

Only a few moments more and Anna came back up the stairs, laughing, singing to herself. When she saw her mother she exclaimed: "Even luck is the servant of a *man!*"

"Is he as small as I thought he was?" asked Rosita, curiously.

"He is not an inch taller than I," said Anna. "He is not ten pounds bigger. He has an eye as soft and blue as the color of a mountain pool. He has a smile like a sleepy child. And a hand faster than a cat's paw. When he stands still he looks like nothing. But whatever he does makes him seem bigger."

"Where are your brothers?"

"Juan has locked himself with a gun into the granary. I can hear him calling on the name of his saint. Pedro I saw running, flopping his arms like the wings of a bat. I saw Miguel crawling on the stones of the patio and begging for mercy because he cannot walk."

"It will do them all good," said the mother. "Some are born to be masters and some are born to be men!"

"The pity of it that he is only an *Americano!*" said Anna.

"Sweet child," said Rosita, "real men are of no nation. And so long as they speak Spanish, do not look the gift horse in the mouth but thank God for your good fortune!"

"Speak Spanish? He can sing it, also," said Anna. "He must be from the opera. And into an old song he puts my name as if he were a poet, too. But; mother, he is in rags."

"Every caballero may be caught in a thorn patch," said the mother. "But what sort of a horse was he riding?"

"Such a horse," said the girl, "that Gil Fanwick will weep blood with envy when he even hears of it. A golden stallion that follows the hand of its master like a sheep dog."

"Now, by the name of kind San Miguel!" said Rosita. "If I were ten years younger and ten inches less around the hips, I would forget the world for a man like that."

"But the rags, mother!"

"Money buys clothes and men buy money," said Rosita. "A wise woman could coin the whole treasury out of one man like this *Americano*. But say your prayers, wash your face clean, and never stop smiling. Who can tell what may happen? What is his name?"

"His name is Sleeper, he says. That is a strange name."

"Men who have strange names have strange stories," said the mother. "Thank God for him and go straight to bed."

16

Operated by fat Carlos Oñate, the cantina on the ground floor of the hotel served patrons who came to sit at the little tables on the side of the street under a row of pepper trees. Carlos served various drinks of Mexican sort but he had also some good American beer which was cooled by a running spring that pooled its waters in Oñate's cellar and then came out sparkling to run down the gutter of the street. Almost the only municipal effort of the town of San Miguel had been to enlarge the gutter to a trough, here and there, so that horses and mules and goats and cattle could be watered up and down the street. And at a table under a pepper tree sat Sleeper, on this bright, hot morning, listening to the trickle and chiming of the spring water and sipping his glass of beer as though time mattered no more to him than it did to the sailing buzzards high over the town.

They seemed to think that San Miguel was dying, and Sleeper appeared willing to be included in the death.

When he lifted his dreaming face from his drink, it was to look through the branches of the trees towards the upper peaks of the Diablo Mountains, glimmering slopes of gray stone on which streaks of dull foliage appeared like thin clouds.

A man rose from an adjoining table, a tall, elderly man with a fat puff of a face and deep blue pouches beneath the eyes. He had legs so long and a body so short and thick that he looked like a great blue crane, and as he rose, he tossed his newspaper aside. It fell at Sleeper's feet, and Sleeper picked it up and seemed, in his mild way, to be offering it back to the older man. Instead, he was saying, softly: "What is it, Colonel?"

"Read the paper. The job's off. Douglas is in hell. Lowry wants you back," muttered the Colonel, and strode away to his horse, which he mounted and rode off down the street.

Sleeper unfolded the paper thoughtfully. The news he wanted was spilled across the front page of the little countryside journal:

STANLEY DOUGLAS ACCUSED
OF TRAIN ROBBERY

The story ran for columns. Sleeper slipped his eye through it rapidly. Four bandits had stopped the Overland, forced the fireman to flood the firebox of the engine, kept the passengers in the coaches, and then cracked open the safe in the mail coach. The theft was nearly seventy thousand dollars. The thieves were unknown with one exception. That exception was very odd, because one of the criminals had actually adressed a companion as "Stan Douglas!"

The man so addressed had the height, the bulk, the

apparent youth of Stanley Douglas—and since his mask was badly arranged, some blond hair showed, like the hair of Stanley Douglas. To make matters certain, it was discovered that Stanley Douglas, after quarreling with his father, had left home. He had turned, apparently, straight to a career of crime!

No wonder Lowry wanted Sleeper to return from this lost cause. For even if young Douglas were returned to his father's house, now, it would be as a dodging fugitive pursued by the law. Stan Douglas must be left to fulfill his own fate, it appeared.

And yet Sleeper, with calm eyes, continued to dwell on the paper long after he had mastered the details of the account. One of the instructions of the pedler had been to keep Douglas away from crime; and in that he had failed. It hardly mattered to Sleeper that it had been impossible for him to prevent the hold-up; the impossible was exactly what Pop Lowry expected of him— otherwise why should Pop have sent him to the Diablo Mountains, a single man, to execute such a mission?

He knew, in his heart, that Lowry hated him with a profound loathing and that he would almost sooner hear of Sleeper's death than of a coup that won him a million for his hoard. Sleeper had given himself into the hands of Lowry for three long months—his pledged word made him the slave of the pseudo-peddler—and yet now he continued to brood over the paper and gradually dismiss the thought of obeying commands and returning at once to Lowry.

It was not the written account that troubled him; it was the large photograph of Stanley Douglas that filled the center of the first page of the newspaper. It showed a fellow no older than Sleeper—in the early twenties, at most, with a fearless eye and a fine, open, handsome face.

This was the man who had thrown himself to the dogs.

101

He had gone downhill like a rolling stone from the moment when his father refused to pay that trifling debt of honor. The success of the first crime would make the second attempt more callous. There might be bloodshed in that affair. And then Stan Douglas would be hopelessly outside the law.

Anna Oñate came hurrying out and stood before Sleeper with frightened eyes. "How can I tell you, señor? The devils have broken into the stable through the back door which hasn't been open for years. They have taken away your beautiful horse—"

"Well," said Sleeper, "if they've taken the horse, bring me another beer, will you, Anna?" And he sat for another hour at least, slowly sipping the cool beer and thinking.

Swift, thoughtless action is like blind charging in a fight. It brings many broken heads and little else. He had known from the first that Careless could not be exposed with impunity to the air of such a place as San Miguel. Now he was stolen as Pop Lowry had warned —but that was exactly what he expected and wished— because he was reasonably certain that the prize would before long find its way into the hands of Fanwick's outlaws.

At last he paid his bill, gave Anna a tip that made her blush, and went back to the stable.

"As though," she told her mother, "to lose such a horse was a nothing, as though he had a whole herd of better horses at home!"

"A real man," said Rosita, "knows that his feet can carry him where no horse will go! Things will soon happen around San Miguel!"

Behind the stable, Sleeper easily found the trail. Among other hoofmarks, those of Careless were as recognizable to him as the faces of four friends in a crowd of strangers. The trail led straight across the hillside, into a shallow draw, and thence up the stony bottom, out across a rock plateau where almost all sign disappeared. He ran all the way with a swinging, smooth Indian gait that devoured the miles with little effort. Where the trail grew dim, he did not decrease his pace but merely bowed over until his head was hardly higher than his hips. So he read the dull print of the trail left by Careless.

That trail had been laid with care. It doubled back here and there and finally topped a small hill not two miles from the town of San Miguel where it had started. Over the top of the hill, Sleeper saw a picture which halted him at once. He never would have expected such a sight among the naked Diablo Mountains. It was rare as an oasis in a desert—a narrow little valley thronged with trees, the thin gleam of a stream running through the center of the slope, and fine, openfaced meadows that offered excellent grazing. Hobbled horses stirred here and there. Canvas tents appeared under the trees. And he marked a group of men, small with distance, gathered to watch a horse which was fighting its rider, flashing like bright gold in the sun.

That was Careless at work, and they would be good riders indeed if they were able to sit on his back.

Sleeper lay down in the shadow of a rock and drew out a spy glass. It was small and light but the lens was excellent. It picked up the distant picture and enlarged it wonderfully. Features of the men were dim, but the whole course of the action was perfectly plain. One rider went off, sailing sidewise. A second followed, a moment later. A third went the same way—a fourth. And yet Careless had hardly opened the box of tricks which his master had taught him. He had not galloped under trees that had low branches. He had not hurled himself to the ground, half-risen, dropped back again. He was merely executing some ordinary maneuvers which Sleeper had taught him to go through with the whirling speed of a fine dancer. And Sleeper, as he watched, laughed a little.

Then he left his place beside the rock and moved rapidly down the side of the valley. High above the middle of the secluded place rose a huge pinnacle of rock on which a single watcher sat turning ceaselessly this way and that. He was a sufficient sentinel to keep guard over the entire crew, except that he was watching for horsemen and not for creatures that moved with the snaky subtlety of Sleeper from shadow to shadow.

When Sleeper was within a hundred yards of the group of men he paused in a thick clump of brush and, worming his way through it, crouched again to make observations. He could read every face, now, with his glass. Three or four men sat about or reclined, badly knocked out by the falls they had received. Careless, sweat-blackened, still shone brightly in the sun—and now there was a pause in the struggle.

It continued until a tall young fellow stepped out from the rest. A shout greeted him, the sound tingling up to where Sleeper waited in concealment. Studying the face of the newcomer with care, he made out the features that he had seen in the newspaper. It was big Stan Douglas.

A little, thin-faced man stood at the stallion's head, steadying Careless before the new attempt was made. When he spoke and made gestures, other men hurried to do his bidding. It was no doubt that famous man, that infamous criminal, the great Gil Fanwick.

As Douglas mounted, Sleeper gave the signal. It was a whistle high and shrill and thin, such as one hears when the scream of an eagle is blown down the wind. The pitch was too high, at such a distance, to run more than the slightest thread of sound through a human ear, but Sleeper could be sure that the stallion's pricked ears would hear it.

The great horse was whirling the instant that his head was released. Instead of using efforts to pitch Douglas from his back, he bolted straight across the floor of the valley towards the source of that whistle—and a yell of triumph came up from the outlaws. They took it for granted that Careless at last was mastered.

Douglas seemed to feel the same thing. He was laughing with joy and making no effort to take a hard pull at the reins. Perhaps Fanwick had offered permanent possession of the horse to the one of his men that could ride it.

But as the chestnut headed straight for the clump of big brush and whirled around the side of it, Careless made one sharp pitch in the air that sent the surprised Douglas out of the saddle. He landed with a heavy thud, sitting on the ground almost at Sleeper's feet.

17

The impact stunned Douglas for a moment while Sleeper lifted his two guns. But the first shock did not endure. Stan Douglas came off the ground like a flame and, since he had no better weapons, went at Sleeper with his hands. He leaped in with a boxer's long, straight shooting left, the most unavoidable of blows, in which the arm strikes out like a long rapier.

And Sleeper met this attack with his hands open and a thoughtful expression on his face. His head swayed a little to the right—the driving fist whirred over his shoulder as he stepped in and struck with the edge of his palm. It is a little trick that has no use unless one knows where to find nerve centers. This blow fell on the strained side of Douglas' neck where all the tendons were drawn stiff. If the shock had been delivered with the edge of an ax the effect could hardly have been more complete. Douglas' head dropped limply on his breast. He lunged straight ahead, but with buckling knees, and would have fallen on his face if Sleeper had not caught him.

Then Stan Douglas, staring helplessly at the gun in the hand of the stranger, was at a loss for words.

"Sit down," said Sleeper.

Douglas shook his head. "Who are you?" he demanded.

"Most people call me Sleeper," was the answer. "Sit down, Stan, and be easy. I'm not an officer of the law and I don't want you for that Overland robbery."

Douglas blinked, then drew in a long breath.

"Then what the devil are you after?" he demanded.

"You," said Sleeper. "You're going home. Home to your father."

"The sheriff would have me the next day," Douglas growled. "What are you driving at?"

"When you held up the train, nobody was killed? There wasn't any bloodshed?" asked Sleeper.

"I'm not talking about the train. I don't know anything about it," said Douglas. "I wasn't there. Somebody else that looked like me—"

"Quit it," urged Sleeper, without heat. "I haven't got the time to argue with you. I could take you in the way you are and get the reward. They've got a reward on your head now, Stan. You know that?"

Stan Douglas said nothing. He could only stare. The big stallion, coming to Sleeper, began to nip cautiously at the brim of his master's old hat. Sleeper put up a hand and pushed the sweating head away.

"You're the man that—" began Douglas.

"They stole the horse from me," said Sleeper. "I could follow any trail that Careless left and I thought it would bring me to Fanwick's gang. And here we are."

"It was you that called him a minute ago?"

"Yes."

"What else can the stallion do? Read books and talk French? I thought I was breaking him," muttered Douglas, ruefully. And suddenly he grinned at Sleeper with a fine flash of his gray eyes.

"You know where the loot is that was taken from the train?" asked Sleeper.

Douglas was silent.

"That's all that stands between you and a cleaner record," said Sleeper. "Return that stuff to the railroad and explain that it was just a foolish practical joke. You know—fool kids running wild. They'll even see a point to the joke if they get the coin back, I think. Or do you want the life down there in the valley? Fanwick and his gang of thieves—do they look good to you?"

Douglas' mouth twisted with distaste. He could not help breaking out: "I've been a damned fool! I've been the biggest fool in the world!"

"Why not wash your reputation clean again, then?"

"You mean, go down on my knees and beg the old man for enough money to pay the railroad back? I'll go to hell, first."

"That's where you'll go, all right, if you don't get the money back. Stan, nobody beats the game. You can't beat the law."

"A fellow can have a few free years, anyway," growled Douglas. "Instead of being kicked around over the map of the world—"

"What kind of freedom?" asked Sleeper. "Taking orders from Fanwick? Is that freedom? Doing his dirty work—is that better than taking orders from your father?"

"I'll never beg for a chance to go back," said Douglas.

"Don't beg, then. Take the chance."

"Take it? How?"

"Have they split up the Overland loot? Is it all together?"

Again Douglas hesitated, staring, but Sleeper's eyes were wide, friendly, and steady. Finally Stan Douglas broke out: "The stuff is still crammed in the saddlebag. Two of the boys haven't come in, yet."

"Then get that saddle-bag," said Sleeper. "Get that and make the run home."

"Get the saddlebag? Out of Fanwick's tent? Hell, even if I were a ghost I couldn't wangle that!"

"I'll help you."

"Look here, stranger. What do you get out of this?"

"Not a penny, if that's what you mean."

"Did father hire you to ride this trail?"

"Your father never heard of me; I never saw him."

"Well it beats me," said Douglas, frowning. "I don't make you out."

"Stay in the dark till you're home—with your hands washed clean."

"And where will you be at the finish?"

"Fanwick will be one down to me."

"You hate Fanwick?"

"Mister Murderer Fanwick? He's not a friend of Sleeper's."

This implied motive seemed enough to satisfy Douglas.

"But the saddle-bag is inside Fanwick's tent, and he never leaves that tent, day or night. He keeps a couple of his best men handy, too. Sawed-off shotguns are lying around."

"Shotguns are never a joke," agreed Sleeper.

"And they're ready to use them," said Douglas. "Every man on Fanwick's inside ring is wanted for more than one murder. They'll shoot to kill."

"It looks a little tough," agreed Sleeper.

"Nothing could be done; unless you had twenty good men. Even then I don't know how the fight would go."

"Numbers won't do it," decided Sleeper. "A crowd would be heard on the way, and the birds would be off. It'll take a light touch and no noise to do this, Stan. What I want to know is this. Will you be with me? If I come down to the camp and try my hand, will you be ready to help? Help steal the money and help make the getaway?"

Douglas turned pale. He pulled out a fresh bandana and rubbed his face with it. He looked down to his freshly polished boots and studied them.

"Yeah," he said, finally.

"Are we shaking on it?" asked Sleeper.

He held out his hand which Douglas, after a bitter inward struggle, forced himself to take. Gradually he lifted his head until his glance held level with Sleeper's.

"I'll be with you," he said at last.

Sleeper said: "If you double-cross me, Stan, I'll manage to live through anything that happens—and get at you!"

He waved a hand to dismiss the subject, and abruptly held out Stan's guns. "Take these back," he said.

The significance of the gesture could not be missed. Douglas, taking the guns, flushed deeply. "All right," he said. "I don't understand you, Sleeper, but I'm starting to appreciate that you're not like any other man."

"God help me, then," answered Sleeper. "When I show up near the camp—where'll I find you?"

"On this side, in a tent under two trees. Spotty sleeps there with me. Be quiet."

"Who's Spotty?"

"A French-Canadian with a long record north of the Border. Knifework is his specialty. He says it makes no sound. And throats cut easier than beef."

"If you hear an owl hoot—two times close together—

like this—" Lowering his head, Sleeper brought from his throat two softly mournful sounds. Though he stood so close, the noise seemed to be drifting from far away. "If you hear that, come out and start for the sound, will you?"

"I will," said Douglas. He repeated the words, sternly, to himself. "I *will* come!"

Sleeper eyed him narrowly, in doubt.

"You've got the right blood in you," he said, "and you'll certainly do better than you think, when the pinch comes. That's when the good blood counts, Stan."

"If I quit on you, I'm the worst skunk in the world!" exclaimed Douglas. "My God, Sleeper, how can you tackle a thing like this for a stranger? And even if you get into the camp, what's your plan to get at the money?"

"I haven't a plan in the world," admitted Sleeper. "I'll try to do some thinking—but remember, day or night, when you hear that old owl hooting, you come for the sound of it."

"I'll come!" repeated the other.

"You've got to ride the horse back, or people may come out chasing him—and pick up my trail."

"Nobody can ride him—except his master," insisted Douglas.

"I'll make it easy for you to ride him. Give me your hand." He placed Stan's hand squarely between the eyes of the big stallion. The horse's ears flattened. He winced back from the touch but slowly straightened again as his master spoke.

"Swing up into the saddle," directed Sleeper.

Douglas obeyed. And the chestnut shrank under the weight like a great cat, a green-eyed danger. Gradually the horse relaxed beneath the voice and the touch of his master.

"You can ride him now," said Sleeper. "Give him a light rein. Talk to him till he gets used to your voice. Talk a lot. He's in your hands, Stan."

Saying that, he stepped back, and watched Douglas ride the stallion slowly out from behind the brush and towards the center of the valley.

18

Anna, starting up suddenly from her place at the window, cried: "I see him!"

"Who?" demanded Rosita.

"I see the señor! Señor Sleeper! I see him walking across the patio, and now through the gate. He turns up the street."

"There's nothing in that," said Rosita.

"Why should he be going out now, in the dusk of the day?" asked Anna. "And at the very time when supper is nearly ready?"

"Men are like cats," said Rosita," and they must walk out in the twilight. They must walk out and smell the night and bristle their whiskers a little—the devils!"

"Señor Sleeper is walking up the street. He comes to the lane—and he turns down it. Why does he turn down that lane? Is it because he has seen that little fool of a Dolores with her loud, squealing laugh and her painted mouth?"

"Girls have the meaning that men choose to give them," said Rosita. "Is he going straight down the lane towards her house?"

"He has come to the bend of the lane—no, he is not walking around it. He stops and looks about him—then he slips into the tall brush!"

"I knew, when I first saw him, that he was a hunting cat," said Rosita. "What bird will he catch in that bush?"

"He has gone through it. He is on the farther side. He looks stealthily about him. He thinks he is alone. He cannot tell that I can look down on him from this height like a bird from the sky."

"Poor bird!" said Rosita. "You are in the sky and yet you are caught if he whistles."

"He begins to run!" exclaimed Rosita. "He disappears into the shallow draw. Now I see only his head as he moves to the west. I am going!"

"Where?"

"After him. How do I know where?"

She turned hastily from the window.

"Don't be a crazy thing," said Rosita. "A woman never can run fast enough to catch a man—it is better to sit still—they run so far that they end up where they begin."

Anna, instead of making an answer, threw open a chest which stood in a corner of the room and snatched out a big new Colt revolver.

"What are you doing with that? Put that back—it's your father's finest gun!" called Rosita.

"If Señor Sleeper needs help, he needs more than my bare hands can give him. Mother, pray for me."

"Hai! Anna! Wait—listen to me!"

But Anna was already off down the steps. Her mother puckered her face and tilted back her head to scream. But she thought better of this and took her stand at the window, looking out over the dim, sunset landscape. She saw Anna cross the patio, turn up the street and into the lane.

At the bend of the lane, the tall girl slipped through the brush and appeared on the farther side of it running like a deer. In fact that slim body of hers was no weight to carry and there was enough Indian blood in her veins to make her as fleet as a rabbit. She ran with a long, easy stride which the short skirt did not impede and in a moment she was out of sight in the shallow draw. Her head did not appear. But her mother knew that the girl was running to the west.

Rosita went back to her sewing and heaved a single sigh. She began to mutter what might have been a prayer—at least she was naming many of the saints.

In Gil Fanwick's camp the darkness had fallen and Fanwick himself had started a pleasant little ceremony. His tent was a fairly comfortable affair with a center table and canvas chairs about it. A bright lantern shone in the center of the table and cast its light over the faces of the four men whom Fanwick had called in. It also gleamed on the canvas side of a saddle bag which reposed on the table, and threw a shadow from it against the faintly luminous wall of the tent.

"This job," said Gil Fanwick, "was one of the smoothest that was ever worked. We should have got away without a trace if Turk Malone hadn't gone out of his head and called Douglas by name. That was simply too damn bad."

"What's become of that fool, Malone?" asked one of the men.

"You'll never see Malone again," said Gil Fanwick. "Nobody else is ever gonna see him. He and I took a ride through the hills, and I came back alone."

The men shifted their glances towards one another. There was no comment. Young Douglas had grown a little pale.

"The rest of you all did well," went on Fanwick, having closed the other subject. "But the rest of you were old hands. Stan Douglas was a green hand. But I take it that he did his stuff."

"He was right on the job," said a redheaded man.

"Cool as steel from the start to the finish," added another.

"He had the hardest part, and he played it well," said

113

Fanwick. "I'm going to give him an extra thousand out of my share."

There was a murmur of hearty agreement. Douglas flushed.

"You know how we have to split this melon, boys?" asked Fanwick. They waited, and he explained: "For the inside tip, I have to pay twenty per cent. You know how it is. We can't work in the dark, and we have to pay high for the sort of news that we want."

"Sure," said Red, "we know that news has to be paid for. But how much is in the sack?"

"Fifty-five thousand," said the chief.

There was a groan, at this. "I thought they said seventy thousand in the papers!" said the youngest of the crew, a kid of nineteen.

"It's a wonder they didn't say a hundred thousand," said Fanwick. "Newspapers live and breed on lies. That's all they are—lies, and lies!" His very color changed with his emotion, but the same senseless, meaningless smile kept twitching his lips. "Twenty per cent to the inside," said Fanwick, continuing, "and one third to me. Does that still hold with you boys?"

"Yeah," said Red. "Or a half. It's equal by me. We'd never make a nickle if you didn't plan the jobs for us."

"Twenty per cent—that's exactly eleven thousand goes out of sight; to a fellow who may have a chance to give us another tip worth twice as much. That's why he has to be paid on the nail. Well, then, that leaves forty-four thousand. A third to me, leaves about twenty-nine. That gives a shade over seven thousand to each of you. How does that sound? Douglas, you get an extra thousand out of my split."

"It sounds small," growled Red. "Here we take and haul in around seventy thousand—according to the papers and what the railroad says. Split that five ways and it would make fourteen thousand for each of us. Now we get down to seven thousand. It looks damn thin to me."

"How about the rest of you?" asked the chief, turning his eye around the circle.

The others shrugged their shoulders. "Let's make the split, Chief," one urged.

"Not a penny," said the leader. "Not till we've talked the whole thing out. I don't want any hard feelings. I won't have them. Either we get along smooth or we don't get along at all."

Douglas spoke, slowly: "As far as I'm concerned, I don't want any extra cut from the chief. I need thirty-five hundred dollars. As long as I get that much, it's as good to me as though I had thirty-five million."

"Because you have a thirty-five hundred dollar debt to pay," said the chief. "Forget that, Douglas. They know your name, now, and they'll slam you in jail for twenty years if they catch you. Forget your debts. You've washed your hands of the old life, debts and everything."

"I can't wash my hands of those things," said Douglas. "They're on my honor."

"Honor? Hell!" said Fanwick. And it was plain that the devil was up in him. "Honor is what men fight for —that and hard cash. The honor goes up the chimney, and the hard cash remains. The crooks that cheated the public two generations ago founded our aristocracy, the fellows that play it big in the headlines today. Honor be damned. Money is what counts in the world. And money is what you boys are going to get. You forget that debt, Douglas."

Douglas said nothing. He was looking steadily into the face of his leader, and it would not have been hard to find words to explain his expression.

"Well, let's make the cut and have it over with," said Red. "I had to say my say, but I'm satisfied. Every man that works with Gil Fanwick gets plenty of coin. There's

115

no doubt about that! By the way, Chief, how much do you lay up in a year?"

Fanwick's face withered. His eyes blinked rapidly before he said: "I pay for horses, chuck, and all sorts of things—guns, ammunition for you to blaze away with. That all comes out of my third, and what I get at the end of a year is a damned sight less than you boys think. But I'm waiting till I get you all ready for the big stuff. The day's coming, boys, when we'll be taking in hundreds of thousands instead of tens. There's millions to be had, and we're going to have them."

He said this with such a fire of conviction that every face lighted except the gloomy face of Stanley Douglas.

Then, very softly from the distant night, came the double hoot of an owl.

Stan Douglas stiffened suddenly, with a quick intake of breath. Only one eye noticed the quick change in him, but that eye was the leader's. He snapped: "Douglas, what the hell does that mean?"

19

Douglas, when he heard the challenge, looked casually over his shoulder. He felt that he was calm all over except in his eyes. He dreaded letting the chief penetrate his mind through those open gates. "Nothing," he said. "Sort of surprised me—that was all—hearing an owl just then."

"It doesn't mean anything to you?" asked the leader.

"No. Of course not," said Douglas, and he turned with a frown. He could feel all eyes on him, prying at his mind; but Fanwick was the only one he feared.

"You're lying!" said Fanwick.

"You can't say that to me," answered Douglas, his fighting blood instantly hot.

Metal winked swiftly into Fanwick's hand. He laid the revolver muzzle on the edge of the table. "Wait a minute, everybody," he said. "Don't move. Listen!"

A moment went slowly by. Then the long drawn, double note of an owl sounded again.

"A damn funny owl that sounds off twice from the same place!" said Fanwick. "Boys, get out of here and walk towards that call. If you sight a two-legged owl on the ground, blaze away with everything you've got." He stared at Douglas. "This is too damn bad," he said. "Don't move a hand, Douglas. If you stir, I'm going to slam lead into you!"

On the verge of the camp, sheltered vaguely behind a small bush, Sleeper had given the signal twice; and now he saw a man coming slowly towards him through the dark. Not one man—for two others moved at a little distance behind the leader.

He had been double-crossed, then, by Douglas, who had betrayed the signal to the bunch! Well, this made it easier, far easier. If Douglas was a skunk, then Sleeper could wash his hands of him and go back to answer the next command of the pseudo-peddler, Pop Lowry.

In the meantime, he had to get out of the way of that trio who moved watchfully, carefully forward. There was not much cover to take. A snake could hardly have used the little irregularities of the ground and the brush, the stones that Sleeper put between himself and the three. Softly, rapidly, on hands and knees, with some wriggling flat on the belly, he drew away. He gained larger brush. He could stand up and run, now, but he had a better thing to do than to run. With his whistle he could bring the great stallion to him. No matter how they had tethered Careless, it would be strange if he could not break away at the call from his master.

Before that whistle shrilled from Sleeper's lips, however, he heard a slight outcry, a scurrying, and then the three pounced on a figure that had risen out of the ground not far from the place where Sleeper had been lying. Then he heard the voice of a girl, the rich, deep voice of Anna Oñate, from the village.

Already they had her far back toward the tent from which they had come. And as the flap of it was thrown back, he saw the light come out and meet her tall body and her high-thrown head. He had hardly seen her before. Now he saw her as though the light shone out of her own mind and body.

Why was she there? Why was she being hauled back before the men in the tent? Who were they?

Douglas, it appeared, had betrayed a new friend. What part had the girl to play in this business?

Sleeper came rapidly back toward the tent. He rounded it to the rear, at the same time hearing a voice that called out, loudly: "What's this girl got to do with it, Douglas? Is she the one that came and made the owl-call for you? Why don't you answer?"

That remark told Sleeper a great deal. He closed in toward the tent. The other men of Fanwick's band—perhaps a dozen of them—were lounging here and there near their own tents, which were scattered under the trees in a sort of oval shape. The tent to which the girl had been brought had, at the front of it, a hitching rack to which four saddled horses were tethered.

Sleeper aimed for them. He untied the ropes that bound them, hearing Douglas say: "I'm not talking. You can think what you want!"

"This is likely to make a hell of a lot of trouble for

118

you!" said the sharp voice of the man who asked the question.

Sleeper, walking slowly, making small whispering noises that caused the horses to prick their ears and come willingly, led the horses around the tent and tethered them to the nearest tree up the slope. As he returned towards the tent, he heard the inquisitor inside it exclaiming: "I'm not going to keep on asking you questions all night long! Will you talk, Douglas?"

There was no answer. Sleeper could feel the strain of the silence. Then, as though rising like a spirit from the ground, a figure appeared suddenly before him, a man with a rifle held at the ready. The fellow had stepped out from the rear of the tent, and Sleeper could understand his own peril and the reason of it. This must be the tent of the leader of the gang. And the leader had chosen to have the back of his tent guarded rather than the face which was exposed to the eyes of all the rest of the band.

"Well?" said the voice of the guard.

Sleeper brought into his hand, with a subtle gesture, the weight of his hunting knife. "Hello, partner," he said.

"You ain't any partner that I remember," said the other, though in the same subdued voice.

"Wait a minute," said Sleeper as he stepped closer. He seemed to be thrusting his face forward, so that it might be seen more clearly.

With the point of the knife he could do his work easily, infallibly. But that would be, in his judgment, murder, even if it were no more than the killing of an outlaw. Therefore he struck, suddenly, for the temple, using only the butt of the knife.

The blow hit the soft of flesh and yielding bone. The guard slumped forward and Sleeper caught the rifle from his hands, lest there should be clattering of metal.

He thrust out his knee and broke the fall of the dropping body, also. Then the man lay still, and Sleeper, on his knees beside him, rapidly tied the hand and feet together and worked a gag inside the teeth.

He was hearing the men inside the tent as this preparation went forward, and above that dominating voice which finally called out: "I won't have any of these damn mysteries. If the girl means something to you, tell me what it is, Douglas."

Sleeper got to the rear of the tent and applied his eye to a very thin rent in the cloth. The scene within was perfectly clear to him, then. He saw the thin, hard face of the leader—he saw Douglas with Fanwick's gun pointed at his breast—he saw Anna Oñate and three men who were watching intently everything that happened.

Douglas said: "I don't know the girl."

"No matter what happens to you, you don't know her?" sneered Fanwick.

Suddenly Anna said: "You do know me, señor. He does know me, Señor Fanwick."

"I thought so," said Fanwick, nodding. "You tell me about it, Anna. You thought he was a pretty fine-looking young fellow, eh?"

"I still think so," said Anna.

"And you let him know that?" demanded Fanwick.

The girl looked at Douglas and suddenly her glance rolled up, and a sort of agony came over her face.

"She's ashamed," said Fanwick, with a sneering laugh. "But I'm about to get to the bottom of this. We're going to find out that Douglas has invited women to come up here—that he's showed the natives where we live. By God, that means that we've all been minutes away from having our throats cut! Murder—that's what it means! Go on, Anna!"

But Anna said: "I meant to help him, Señor Fanwick. I didn't mean to do him any harm!"

"Well, tell me the truth, then."

"Will it take away trouble from this poor young man?" asked the girl.

"We'll see about that," answered the chief.

"I never saw the señor before," said the girl, nodding at Douglas. She was panting with excitement, and her eyes flashed—they were like the eyes of a deer, big, gleaming, accustomed to danger and the escape from it by flight.

"If you never saw Douglas before, what brought you up here?" asked Fanwick.

"Another man," she said.

"Ah ha! Which one!"

"Señor Sleeper!" said the girl, blushing very red.

"Sleeper? Who the devil is that?" demanded Fanwick. "Is that the nickname of one of my men?"

"He is the man with the red stallion," said the girl.

"Ah, that man! Wait a minute! You say that he came up here?"

"Yes, señor."

"When?"

"There's no use trying to follow him. He's gone far away, by this time," said Anna. "And God forgive me! Every man suffers because of what I say!"

"You followed him up here—this night?" shouted Fanwick.

"Yes, señor," said the trembling girl.

Sleeper's pulse struck a note like a drum-beat through his ears. He could hardly believe the thing he heard. But it was spoken under circumstances that could not lead to anything but the truth.

"Get out of here!" called Fanwick to his men. "Douglas, stay here because I've got to talk to you damned straight. The rest of you scatter. Find me this Sleeper and bring him back by the ears, dead or alive!"

Sleeper, lifting the rifle, had aimed it carefully through

121

the small gap in the side of the tent. Now, as the men rose hastily, he pulled the trigger, and with the boom of the gun there came an answering crash of glass, and the lantern went out.

20

One sweep of the hunting knife divided the back of the tent with that razor-edge of sharpness. Inside, there was a swirl of figures, a rapid clattering of exclamations, and from the distance came the shouting of the men who had heard the rifle shot and seen the light extinguished in the leader's tent.

"Douglas!" called Sleeper. "Anna!"

His first answer was a spitting red flame from the muzzle of a revolver. He slashed back with the edge of the knife and the keen edge slashed through flesh and grated on bone. A screech answered the stroke, and two swift figures darted out of the rent in the back of the tent, past Sleeper who had gained the table and seized the saddle-bag.

He was after them like a greyhound. "Straight ahead!" he called, panting. "The tree—the horses there!"

Behind him, glancing over the shoulder, he saw a tumbling knot of figures spilled out from the tent. But they were well behind, and the two ahead of him ran well. Douglas—he noted with a keen and approving eye—would not race on ahead of the girl but kept steadily at her side. And out of Sleeper's lips came a long, shrilling whistle. That signal would be heard by sharper than human ears, and it would be answered unless the restraining ropes were very strong indeed!

They were at the four horses, now, slashing the lead ropes instead of pausing to untie them. In the rear, the sharp, barking voice of Fanwick raved madly. More distant answers proved that orders were being heard and obeyed. The whole number of these men would soon be on horseback, of course, and they would sweep like so many hawks in pursuit of the fugitives.

The girl was first in the saddle, leaping to her place like any active lad. Big Stan Douglas followed. Sleeper was the last to gain a place and take the spare horse on the lead.

Now he saw that there was no further pursuit up the slope. Instead, Fanwick and his men, dropping to their knees or lying flat, were taking pot-shots at the flying shadows as the fugitives went off at a full gallop. Other horsemen were mounting in the hollow of the valley, dimly seen.

And now a form rushed rapidly, as though on wings, up the slope, over taking the three. "Go on, the two of you! I'll take care of that one!" called Douglas. He was reining his horse in, poising a gun, when Sleeper saw a glint of starlight on the pursuing figure.

"Don't shoot!" he cried. "It's Careless coming—and there's no man on his back!"

He came straight on to the second whistle of his master. And Sleeper, swinging out from the saddle, was instantly on the naked back of the stallion. It did not matter that there was no saddle, no bridle. A touch of hand or voice would guide the big horse.

And so they gained the ridge of the hills, while behind them a roar of many hoofs swept up from the floor of the valley. As the three poured over the ridge, outlined for a moment against the stars, a rattle of gunfire rose behind them. It ended as they dipped on the farther side of the hill.

He rode close beside the girl, leaning from his place. And as he leaned he called: "D'you hear, Anna? Turn left! We'll take the right—they'll follow us—they won't follow you—"

She merely looked up and shook her head. She laughed: "This is the best part of the dance, Señor Sleeper!"

The noise of hoofs mounted the ridge. Sleeper looked helplessly down at Anna. He was aware of Douglas riding just ahead, and of the big saddle-bag flopping clumsily at the side of one of the led horses.

Two or three gunshots rang out together—and the girl suddenly was struck double over the horn of her saddle. A bullet had surely found her. She began to slip to the side. Sleeper, pressing the stallion closer, held her in place with one straining hand.

And he called: "Douglas, take the saddle-bag and that lead horse. Go on! Ride like the devil! The girl's hurt— I'll stay with her. If you ride ahead, they'll probably follow you. It's you and that saddle-bag that they want!"

But Douglas was not to be deceived by such talk. There was plenty of manhood in him, and he showed it now. He reined straight back beside the girl and with his powerful hand helped to right her in the saddle.

She recovered from the first shock of the impact and pain. "Sleeper—señor!" she gasped. "Mother of heaven, I am dying!—Señor Sleeper, I cannot sit the saddle. I cannot—"

"You have to!" commanded Sleeper. "Where did the bullet hit?"

"I don't know—I don't know—here—in the shoulder!"

He touched that shoulder and his hand felt the hot wetness of the blood. But there was no great flow of it. The horses were speeding down a shallow valley. Now they were turning onto the broad slope that led down toward the village of San Miguel, far away.

They could not get to the town, he knew, before Fanwick's men would overtake them. He and Douglas—yes, they could escape, but not with the wounded girl to set pace for them. There was no way of dodging. It was all a straight run and the only way of crossing the sharp-sided ravine which cut along the slope of the mountain was to take the bridge which arched the chasm a mile above the town of San Miguel. Toward that point they had to run their horses with the men closing the gap every moment.

It was a matter of moments. The rising wind which blew on their backs seemed no help to them—it was assisting the pursuit only.

"You *can* ride, Anna!" said Sleeper. "Set your teeth hard. Can you move that left arm?"

She tried and nodded, with a groan.

"Then there are no bones broken," he said. "It's a flesh wound. And you can stand it."

"I *can* stand it," she answered suddenly.

He had snatched off his shirt and now he caught this around her body and knotted it behind, so that the wounded arm was pressed close to her side. That would keep it from swinging, and would leave one arm free for clinging to the horse. The reins he took himself.

They made slightly better speed, now, but still the outlaws were gaining. And the tall, dead grass made a rushing sound, like water, about the sweeping legs of the horses.

Douglas called: "There's nothing to do, Sleeper! They've got us before we can reach the bridge. Or, on the other side of the bridge they'll run us down. We're done for. Let's send the girl on and try to hold them back—"

If that was the stuff that Douglas was made of, Sleeper

was glad that he had risked all these chances for the sake of the man.

"We can't leave her—because she won't go!" called Sleeper in answer.

"Then there's nothing to be done—and we're lost!" cried Douglas. "By God, Sleeper, I've dragged the two of you down into hell!"

Sleeper, glancing desperately around him, saw the whirling bright faces of the stars overhead, listened to the noise of the hoofs in the grass and heard the shrilling of the storm which was whipping their backs. Dead grass and a high wind right on the course towards San Miguel—

"There's a chance!" he shouted.

And leaning from the back of the horse, he caught up handful after handful of the tall, brittle grass. He twisted it hard into a tight ball. Then, holding it down before him on the saddle, he fished a wooden match from his pocket, snapped the head with his thumbnail. Dry as the grass was it took four matches before he managed to ignite the grass—and then, instantly, it puffed flame into his face, so powder-dry was the old growth. Quickly he flung the ball of fire into the long grass behind him and spurred on.

A thin column of smoke rose, and a dark red tongue of the flame. The flame spread. The wind caught a billow of it, tossed it far ahead, and a fresh fire burst out violently.

Fanwick's men reached the point of ignition. The flames rose from it in a cloud of sparks and luminous smoke and fire. As fast as the wind, that fire blew and spread. The height of it increased, the noise of its roaring reached the ears of the fugitives, and the red sparks began to shower over them.

Fanwick's men were spreading out to the right and to the left to round the course of the fire, but it shouldered still farther out and drove them back. And straight behind Sleeper and his two companions the sea of flame rolled down for the bridge that crossed the chasm.

They crossed that bridge, the three of them, not half a dozen jumps ahead of the front of the wall of flame. As they rode on, they could see torrents of crimson light flooding their path—and all sight and sound of the outlaws was lost well behind them.

They were safe. The crowd in San Miguel would give them a sufficient protection once they reached that haven. And beyond it they could ride on, when the girl was safe at her home again. When they looked back from close to the town, they could still see the red inferno raging behind the canyon. It had done its job well.

Then they were in the still street of San Miguel, hushed as sleep at this time in the night. They came to the hotel, and Sleeper rapped on the patio gate. Behind him, big Stan Douglas was holding the girl in his arms, because she had fainted dead away.

A window screeched up. The voice of Rosita called: "Who is there?"

"Sleeper!" was the answer. "And your daughter—"

A wild cry of excitement answered him. The window slammed down. Footfalls rattled on the stairs. They clattered on the stone pavement of the patio. The gáte was unlocked and wrenched open.

"Your daughter's hurt—wounded in the shoulder," said Sleeper. "But she'll get better, well enough. Don't doubt that. There's no man in the world with a better nerve or a truer heart."

"Hai!" cried Rosita. "Anna—you hear me?"

"Faster!" murmured the girl. "Faster! Ah, God, they are turned back by the fire—even fire is his servant—"

Sleeper took her from Douglas and carried the slim body up the stairs.

21

The doctor came at once; at Anna's wound he merely laughed. Two days in bed and a nourishing diet would make up for the blood she had lost.

"She was no nearer to death than thinking of it," said the doctor.

And in the meantime, outside the bedroom door, in the dingy hall by lantern-light Sleeper was saying goodbye to big Stan Douglas. "You've had enough freedom," he said. "Go back and square yourself with the railroad. Call the thing a joke. They'll laugh and pat you on the back."

Douglas nodded. "I'll do that," he agreed. "And if my father wants to kick me in the face—why, that's what my face is for! But what about you, Sleeper? What are you going to do after this?"

"Whatever the devil tells me to," said Sleeper.

"The devil? The devil never was inside your mind, old fellow!"

"The devil is the one who sends me out on the trail," said Sleeper. "I have ten weeks of his special hell ahead of me. If I live through that—"

He made a gesture and whistled. Then they shook hands.

Afterward, Sleeper sat beside Anna's bed. He held one of her hands and looked straight down into her eyes.

"Have you ever heard of the town of White Water?" he asked.

"I know where it is," said the girl.

"If there's ever a time when you need help—you or

your family," said Sleeper, "send to White Water and find an old peddler called Pop Lowry. He'll know where to find me."

"And you," said the girl, "are you going there now?"

"Yes," said Sleeper. "I'll write to you soon. I'll have news for you, Anna."

"You'll never come back," said the girl.

"I? Of course I'll come back!" said Sleeper.

"Go—quickly—" said the girl. "Before I begin to cry."

And Sleeper went—quickly, silently in his moccasined feet.

Rosita said, when he had left: "You might have held him longer than that, Anna! Where was your tongue? Suppose that he had seen a few tears? Men like to remember them!"

"I'm glad he's gone," answered Anna. "You, mother, are a wise woman. You know a great deal more than any three men in San Miguel. You should be glad that he's gone, also!"

"Why?" asked the mother.

"Do you remember what you told me: that wild-caught hawks fly better than tame ones?"

"I remember."

"Why did you say that?" Anna asked.

"Because they're used to living on the wing."

"That is true of Sleeper, also," said the girl. "All other men are tame. They have weak wings. They are nothing. But Sleeper has flown so high that he'll never come down to earth to a girl like Anna. So I'm glad that he has gone away forever."

"Nevertheless," said the mother, "you'll hear from him at least once more."

They did hear from him, and by something much weightier than a letter. A week or more later a muleteer brought to the hotel a loaded mule and left it in the charge of Anna herself as she sat in the cool of the evening at the cantina. She was already forgetting Sleeper—the lads of San Miguel had such bright eyes, such charming smiles!

But when the pack was taken from the mule's back— when on the tables were unloaded muslins, silks, laces, and bright slippers, and figured cloths, and packets of feathers for hats, and strings of brilliants and rare beads—when she saw these things and gradually realized that they were all meant for her, Anna's heart overflowed and she wept with joy.

"So you see," said Rosita, "that a mother's eye is the sharpest. I knew that good would come out of him, after all! And the blood you've lost has only been enough to wash the wish for him out of your heart. Look—there are even rings and bracelets! Mother of heaven, the cost of that mule-load must be two, three thousand dollars! What a prince among young men! What a hero! What a good man!"

Anna opened the little note that came with the great gift and read, merely:

> When all that the mule brings is worn out, I shall still be remembering you.

"There," said Rosita, "is the speech of a gentleman. To love a man like that—it is much better than the reading of a good book!"

And Anna agreed.

Far north of San Miguel, near the town of White Water, at that very moment Sleeper was reading a newspaper which carried, not on the first page but toward the center of the news, this item:

> Railroad robbery was joke! Stanley Douglas returns money taken from Overland!

Sleeper looked up from the page.

"But it's not a joke—not the money Stan's father paid to you, Pop?"

130

Pop Lowry was on his knees, arranging the stuffs which he was putting into one of the panniers for his trade among the ranchers.

He said: "A joke? The money I took from that man was given to me with a smile and a handshake. Old Douglas tells me that his son has given him the whole story. Old Douglas wants you to come and stay at their home. He says that Stan is a new man. It is all owing to you. That is what they say. But what about Pop Lowry, who gave you the news and the opportunity? What about me? I get no thanks, only money!"

"How much money?" asked Sleeper, curiously.

"Well, he's a rich man," said the pedler. "It was to have been twenty thousand dollars; but after Stan became a robber—why, I boosted the price several notches."

"To what?" asked Sleeper.

"What do you care?" snapped the pedler. "I gave the mule-load of nonsense to the Mexican girl for you, and that's all you asked for yourself."

Sleeper sighed.

"And tomorrow," said Pop Lowry, "I have new things for you to do. Go to bed early tonight. You'll be riding Careless in the morning."

22

Sleeper was hungry. There was plenty of game to be shot in the mountains around him but he had neither rifle nor revolver. He had not even a fishing line or a fishhook. He might build traps to catch rabbits or the stupid mountain grouse. But that would require a day or more of work and waiting, and he was too hungry for that.

So he found a shallow stream where the sun struck through the rapid of water and turned the sands to gold. There, on a flat ledge of rock just above the edge of the stream, he stretched himself and waited. Only a thin sliver of his shadow projected into the tremor of the water, and his blue eyes grew fierce with hunger when he saw the trout nose their way up stream leisurely in spite of the swift tumbling of the little brook.

They moved in their element with perfect ease, like birds in the sky. One that looked sluggish with bigness and fat disappeared in a twinkling and a flash when Sleeper's lightning hand darted down to make the catch.

But his patience was perfect. If a bear can lie on a bank and knock salmon out of a creek, Sleeper could lie in the same manner and flick out a trout now and then. He not only supposed so but he knew it, because he had done the thing many times before in the famine days of his boyhood.

His deceptively slender body remained motionless. Nothing about him stirred except the blue glinting of his eyes. And in them was the sign of the gathered nervous tension, the piling up of electric force ready to work with the speed of a leaping spark when the moment came to make a contact.

Another speckled beauty drifted up the stream at lordly ease. The fish started to dissolve in a flash, but the darting hand of Sleeper flicked through the water and from his fingertips the trout was sent hurtling high into the air, to land in the grass well up the bank.

At the lower verge of the trees which descended the mountainside and stopped a little distance above the creek, Pop Lowry halted his three packmules and looked out on the scene below. He began to smooth his bald head and laugh, silently as a grinning wolf, when he saw this fishing going on. Yet he remained there, screened by the trees and brush, while Sleeper stood up from his rock and started to make a small fire. Expertly Sleeper cleaned the fish and broiled them over the handful of flame. He was still busy when he called out: "Why don't you show your ugly mug, Pop? I'm used to it. It won't hurt my feelings."

Pop Lowry, with a start, came suddenly out from among the trees, hauling at the lead-rope of the first mule, to which the other pair were tethered. Two big panniers wobbled at the sides of this mule; heaping packs swelled above the backs of the others. Pop Lowry, shambling down the slope in his clumsy boots, waved a greeting to Sleeper, and as he came up, he said: "How come, Sleeper? What you done with thirty thousand dollars in three days, boy? Or was it a whole week?"

A dreaming look came into Sleeper's blue eyes. Then he smiled. "If that red horse had won Saturday," said he, "I'd be worth a quarter of a million!"

"What red horse?" asked Pop. His long, pock-marked face kept grinning at Sleeper, but his eyes narrowed and brightened as they strove to pierce into the nature of the youth.

"He's a thoroughbred, Pop," said Sleeper. "And he should have won. I put my money on him over at the rodeo and watched it go up in smoke."

"You mean that you bet all that on one horse—on one race?" demanded Pop.

"You know how it is," said Sleeper. "It's better to stay dirty poor than be dirt rich. I mean—what's thirty thousand?"

"It's fifteen hundred a year income, if you place it right," declared Pop Lowry.

"If I'm going to have money, I want real money," answered Sleeper. "He was only beaten by a head, so I don't mind."

He began to eat the broiled fish, while Pop looked on

in a peculiar combination of horror and delight.

Sleeper was succeeding in that task very well while the peddler filled a pipe and lighted it, then sat down on a stump to smoke.

"Supposin' that you got that two hundred and fifty thousand dollars, Sleeper, what would you do with it?" Pop asked.

"I'd get married," said Sleeper. "But I don't know who I'd marry."

"You'd get married—and you don't know to what girl?" shouted Lowry. "Doggone me if you ain't a crazy one!"

"I don't know which one," said Sleeper. "There's Kate Williams—I get pretty dizzy every time I think about her. But then there's Maisry Telford. And her eyes have a way of smiling that I can't forget."

"Maisry Telford—why, she ain't nothin' but a little tramp. She ain't got a penny to her name," said the peddler. "But you mean that Kate Williams would take you, Sleeper?"

"Perhaps she wouldn't," said Sleeper, "but there have been times when we seemed to understand each other pretty well."

"My God, she's worth a coupla millions," said the peddler. "At least, when her father dies, she is. Marry her, kid, if you got any sense at all. Maisry Telford, what's she got?"

"A good pair of hands on reins or a rifle, and a nice way with a horse or a man. She could ride all day and dance all night. She doesn't need a big house. She's at home in the whole range of the mountains. She could find you a rabbit stew in the middle of the desert, and she could find firewood above timberline in a thirty below blizzard. That's some of the things that she could do."

"Take her, then," said the peddler. "It ain't in you to have sense and marry money. It ain't in you to keep anything. What you got on you now?"

"A comb, a toothbrush and a razor," said Sleeper. "A bridle and saddle and a horse to wear them; clothes to cover me; and a knife so that I can carve my name right up on the forehead of this little old world, Pop."

Pop Lowry began to laugh. "If I was a magician and could give you any wish, what would you ask for first?"

"A sack of bull and some wheatstraw papers," said Sleeper.

Pop Lowry, laughing still, opened one of the hampers of his first mule and produced the required articles. Sleeper accepted them with thanks, and soon was smoking.

"Why did you want me to meet you up here?" asked Sleeper. "I've been waiting a whole day."

"I was held up," said the peddler.

"What sort of crookedness held you up?" demanded Sleeper. "Were you planning a bank robbery, or just to stick up a stage? Or were you bribing a jury to get one of your crooks out of jail?"

"Sleeper," said the peddler, "it's a kind of a sad thing the way you ain't got no faith in me. But the thing that I want you to do now is right up your street. It's just the breakin' of a hoss to ride."

"What kind of a horse?"

"Just a nervous sort of a high-headed fool of a stallion," said the peddler. "And four of my boys have tried their hands with him and gone bust."

"Where'd you steal the horse?" asked Sleeper.

"There you go ag'in!" sighed Pop Lowry, "as though I never bought and paid for nothin' in my life. But lemme tell you where the place is. You know Mount Kimbal? Well, down on the western side there's a valley, small and snug with Kimbal Creek running through it. And back in the brush there's a cabin . . ."

"Where the Indian lived that Tim Leary killed," said Sleeper.

"Right. Go there, Sleeper. You'll find the hoss there.

135

You'll find Dan Tolan there, too; and Joe Peek and Harry Paley and Slats Lewis. Know them?"

"No."

"You'll know 'em when you see 'em. Tell 'em I sent you."

"I just break the horse, is that all?" asked Sleeper.

"Wait a minute. The thing is to break that hoss to riding, and to deliver his reins into the hands of a gent named Oscar Willis in the town of Jaytown. That's all you have to do, and them four will help you to do it."

"Where's the catch?" asked Sleeper.

The peddler hesitated, his small bright eyes shifting on Sleeper's face.

"There's some two-legged snakes that would like to have that hoss to themselves," he said at last. "You'll have to keep your eyes open."

"How does it happen that you've never given me murder to do?" asked Sleeper, looking with disgust at the pock-marked face of the peddler. "While I'm a sworn slave to you for six weeks or so longer, how does it happen that you haven't asked me to kill somebody?"

"Why ask a cat to walk on wet ground?" said the peddler. "Why give you a murder to do and let you hang afterwards? In the first place you wouldn't do the job, no matter how you've swore to be my man for the time bein'. In the second place, there's other errands you can run to hell and back for me!"

23

Dan Tolan was big, not above six feet, perhaps, but built all the way from the ground, up to ponderous shoulders and a bull neck, to a jaw that was capable of breaking ox-bones to get at the marrow inside them. Above the jaw, big Dan Tolan sloped away. The executive part of his body was constructed along the most generous lines; but the legislative chamber was small. He had little or no forehead, and the structure of his skull was pyramidal from behind, also, sloping upwards and inwards from the great bulging fleshy wrinkles at the top of his neck.

Big Dan Tolan, standing at the door of the shack with a rifle in his hands, looked with disfavor at the slender young man who stood before him.

Looking past this stranger, Dan Tolan saw the horse which had carried the other to the spot, and the heart of Dan was burning with desire. Every line of that creature spoke of speed and breeding. He was sixteen hands high if he was an inch, and muscled in a way that promised even the weight of Dan Tolan a ride.

"Who are you? Whatcha want? Who sent you?" asked Tolan.

"Sleeper. To break the stallion. Lowry," said Sleeper.

Tolan blinked. Then he realized that his triple question had been answered part by part.

"Lowry?" he repeated. There was no comment from Sleeper. "So Pop Lowry sent you, eh?" said Tolan. Then, without turning his head, he called, "Hey, fellers, come out there."

They came to the door. Slats Lewis was enormously tall, vastly thin, with a pair of ears like the wings of a

137

bat, but the other two were not remarkable in any way. They would never have been noticed in any large crowd of cowpunchers.

"This here," said Tolan, "was sent by Pop. What the hell you think of that? To break the stallion, he says!"

The face of Slats was split in two by a gaping grin. "Give him a try," said Slats. "And—*where* did he get that red hoss, yonder?"

"Leave that hoss alone. I seen it first," said Tolan. "You want to try your hand at the stallion, eh?"

He began to grin and rub his left hip with a caressing hand. And Sleeper took note of a bandage around Slats' head, and a great purple bruise which disfigured Mister Joe Peek's forehead. Harry Paley had all the skin off the end of his nose, and it was not the heat of the sun which had removed it.

"Sure, and why not leave him have a try at Inverness?" asked Paley.

In his eagerness, he hurried out and led the way around the side of the shack to a corral which had been newly built, and which consisted of strong saplings which had been planted in a wide circle, and strengthened with cross-pieces. It made a living corral of trees with one narrow gate.

Inside that corral was one of the finest animals that Sleeper had ever seen—a thoroughbred bay stallion.

"Walk right in and make yourself at home," said Paley.

Sleeper climbed one of the trees and sat out on a lower branch. Inverness, having apparently turned his back to the stranger and lost all interest in him, whirled suddenly, crossed the corral with a racing stride, and bounded high into the air. His eyes were two red streaks; and his mouth gaped like that of some carnivorous beast.

But he fell just short in his effort, and his teeth snapped vainly at Sleeper's leg.

There was a yell of applause from the other four.

"Come down and tackle him on his own ground," yelled Dan Tolan.

But Sleeper merely crossed his legs and rolled a smoke.

"Leave him be," said Paley. "He wants to think a while, and I guess I know what he's got in his bean, all right."

"We don't need to wait for the show to start," commented Slats. "When the circus begins, the band'll start up, all right."

They went back to the shack, muttering vague comments about Pop Lowry, who had sent them a half-wit, a baby-face to do a man's work. Yet it was very, very odd, for Pop was not the fellow to make important mistakes.

They first looked over the golden stallion which had brought the youth to them. There were plenty of features that were worth much observation. For one thing, instead of a bridle the horse wore merely a light hackamore; he was guided, it appeared, without a bit at all.

"Just one of these here family pets," said Slats.

"Look out. I never seen a stallion that was no family pet," said Paley.

"I'll ride him," declared Slats.

Slats was far the best rider of them all, and they helped him put on the saddle and cinch it up. The lack of a bit troubled Slats a little, but he declared that he would have no trouble with the stallion.

In fact, the big golden beauty—which would have made almost twice the substance of racy Inverness—stood as quietly as a family pet while the saddle was being adjusted and even when Slats swung into the stirrups.

After that the great stallion, Careless, did a dancing step and turn, with a whipsnap at the end of it, and Slats slid out into the air and came down in a sitting posture with a great thump.

Careless resumed his grazing; he showed not the slightest desire to bolt. Slowly Slats got to his feet.

"Anybody *see* that kid ridin' this here?" asked Slats.

"No," said Tolan.

"Then he never *did* ride him. He brought him up here on a lead. There might be one man in the world that can ride that devil, but there ain't two."

"Hold on, Slats," said Tolan. "Ain't you gonna try agin?"

"Me? I've had enough tryin'," said Slats, and stalked back into the house.

The others stripped off the saddle again, and Careless kept his ears pricked as he grazed.

"There's somepun behind all this here," declared Tolan. "Two hosses that can't be rode. And Lowry behind the both of them. What might it mean, anyway?"

"Go see how the kid's getting on with Inverness," said one.

Paley went and came back with the report that the kid had descended from his tree and now was sitting on the ground. "*Inside* the corral!" said Paley.

There was a general exclamation of wonder. "How come?" demanded Tolan.

"I dunno how come," answered Paley. "But he's sure settin' there smokin' cigarettes and talkin' none at all. Just whistling a little. Lullaby songs is what he's whistling. Maybe he thinks Inverness is a baby in a cradle."

They laughed a good bit at this and went back to their poker game inside the shack. As the dusk came on and they lighted a lantern, Tolan went out to the corral.

"You don't eat none 'till you're rode that hoss!" he shouted.

Then, coming close to the corral, he peered between the trunks of the trees and saw a sight that made the hair lift on his head. A tiny spot of light caught his eye, first, and then in the dimness beneath the trees he was able to make out a slender form seated on the bare back of Inverness!

It was true. There sat Sleeper on the unsaddled back of Inverness, sometimes puffing a cigarette which faintly lighted his handsome face, and sometimes whistling plaintive little songs.

And the stallion, moving slowly, still grazing the short grass inside the big corral, paid no heed whatever to the burden on his back.

Dan Tolan went back to the shack and stood breathless with astonishment on the threshold.

"Him—Sleeper—he's on the back of that damned hoss—and Inverness *likes* it!" he gasped.

There was a general springing up.

"Set that table for five," said Tolan, "because as far as I see, the kid is gonna eat with the men tonight."

There was a good deal of clattering about the old stove which stood in a corner of the shack, and more jangling in setting out the tin plates and cups on the table. But through this noise, a little later, the voice of Sleeper sounded.

"All right, boys," he said. "I guess Inverness is ready to be delivered."

They poured out from the shack, and found that Inverness, saddled and bridled, was dancing in the starlight before the cabin. Around him, prancing, rearing as though to strike, maneuvered the great, gleaming body of Careless.

"Go back—back!" called Sleeper.

Careless went rapidly back, snorting protest.

"Lie down, boy," called Sleeper.

And the four staring men saw the stallion sink to the ground as though he had been a well-trained hunting-dog.

And now Sleeper rode Inverness softly back and forth, saying: "He's been broken to the bridle. He's been managed long ago. He just has to remember a few things, and then he'll be safe for a lady to ride to church."

141

24

When Sleeper sat at the table with the others, Dan Tolan said to him: "How you come to handle hosses like that? Got some Injun in you, or something?"

"Hey, he's got blue eyes, ain't he?" interrupted Harry Paley. "How could he be an Injun?"

"Yeah, and I've seen blue-eyed Injun-breeds," said Dan Tolan, scowling heavily at Sleeper. "Or maybe you got some greaser in you, kid?"

"Look for yourself," said Sleeper smiling.

He showed his white teeth as he smiled. It was almost caressing but just a trifle feline and dangerous.

"What you mean look for myself?" demanded Dan Tolan, pouring half a cup of steaming black coffee down his great gullet.

He wiped his mouth on the back of his hand and left a dirty stain clinging to the stiffness of the hairs.

"Why, a fellow ought to be able to tell what other people are by giving them a look," said Sleeper.

"Yeah, and how would I know what you done to Inverness?"

"I waited till the evening came on," said Sleeper. "Horses are like men. They get lonely at the end of the day, and when Inverness poked his head over the fence and tried to look his way out of trouble, I talked to him a little."

"Now, listen to the crazy talk this kid is throwing," said Slats, and split his face exactly in half with a grin.

"He *talked* to Inverness, eh?" laughed Paley.

"I talked till I got his ears forward. Then I went inside the corral," said Sleeper. "The rest was easy. When he didn't smash me up in his first charge, I saw that he

142

wasn't a mean horse. He'd only been misunderstood."

"He'd only been *what?*" roared Slats. "Listen to me. I was short and fat till he slammed me on the ground so hard that he made me what I am today. You mean that was because I misunderstood him?"

"Misunderstood!" murmured Dan Tolan. Then he roared out: "You went and hypnotized him—or you give him some dope. Why don't you open up and try to tell the truth like a man? What did you do to the hoss, I'm asking?"

"We had a little talk together, and then I hopped up on his back. He didn't mind at all. It just reminded him of the old days."

"What old days?" asked Dan Tolan. The other three straightened a little in their chairs.

"The old racing days," said Sleeper.

"I suppose the hoss told you that he used to be a racer?" asked Paley.

"That's right," said Sleeper. "There's a saddle mark on Inverness."

"That's a lie!" exclaimed Dan Tolan. "There ain't no mark of no kind at all on him. I been over him inch by inch."

"With your eyes, not with your hands," said Sleeper. "There's a soft saddle mark behind the withers. I felt it across the bone. A Western saddle, a regular range saddle, doesn't sit where an English saddle sits," Sleeper explained. "Inverness is a racer and a good one. He's a stake horse—or he ought to be."

The other four stared at one another.

"He's kidding us," said Dan Tolan, presently. "Run your hands over Paley. Tell us something about him, will you?"

"He'd be more at home working a faro lay-out," said Sleeper.

"Hey! Hold on!" exclaimed Paley.

"Aw, he seen you somewhere at work," said Dan Tolan. "What about Joe Peek? What's the touch of Joe tell you?"

"Joe sang around in bar rooms and maybe at the Bird Cage theater till his voice went back on him," said Sleeper.

"Now—I'll be damned!" muttered Peek. "He never seen *me* on the stage, anyway!"

"How you come to guess that?" asked Tolan, scowling in darker anger than before.

"Why, he hummed one of the songs a while ago," said Sleeper. "One of those 'love you till the seas run dry' songs. And he has a husky voice—like a singer that took to liquor instead of singing lessons. Besides, he keeps his clothes clean, ties his bandana with a fancy knot, looks at his boots as though he expected to see them shine . . . and real good singers don't spoil their voices with redeye" Sleeper wound up.

There was a silence. Peek was glaring. Then Tolan laughed. "Go on, kid," he said. "Try Slats. What's he been?"

"Murder," said Sleeper, and looked straight across the table at Slats. The tall man stared back, his eyes pale and bright.

"By God," whispered Slats, "who are you?"

He pushed back his chair, softly, keeping those hypnotic, pale eyes steadily on Sleeper's face.

"Leave him be," interrupted Tolan. "You done pretty well with the rest. Now what about me?"

"Before you entered the ring, or after you left it?" asked Sleeper.

Tolan started. "What—" he began. Then he paused and went on: "You could tell that by the marks on my face, maybe."

"You could of got those in barroom fights," said Paley. "No, he figgered it some other way. How, Sleeper?"

"He looks at a man's hands instead of at his eyes," said

144

Sleeper. "He steps short; he's light on his feet in spite of his weight; and he seems set to punch when he stands close to a man. Besides . . ."

"That's enough," said Paley. "Want some more, Dan?"

"Yeah?" muttered Tolan. "Why not? What else you think you know, kid?"

"It's a long yarn, I guess," said Sleeper, "and I'm tired of talking."

"*I* ain't tired," answered the big fellow. "Go and yap your damned piece and let's hear what's in it?"

"Women—and a good deal of dirt," said Sleeper.

"Ha!" grunted Dan Tolan, pushing back his chair in his turn.

"Wait a minute," said Slats, grinning as he laid a restraining hand on his leader's shoulder.

"Yeah. I'm O.K.," said Tolan. "Leave him talk. I wanta hear him yap!"

"When the easy money played out, you got into some trouble that landed you in the pen," said Sleeper. "That's why you were never beaten in the ring. You got into the juzgado first."

There was one burst of laughter that died at once. The men were watching the white hate in the face of Tolan, and it silenced them.

"And then, afterwards, you didn't give a damn," said Sleeper. "You felt that the world owed you something, and you took it with a gun. Then you got thick with Slats and since then you've been pointing out to him the fellow it was worth shooting—sometimes you even help with the killings. And if . . ."

Tolan rose to his feet, slowly.

"Wait a minute," protested Slats. "Don't go and beat him up, chief, till you find out who told him these things."

"How do you tell a skunk from a coyote? By the look of the face, mostly," said Sleeper. "Slats wears his guns so that I could hardly spot them—he's a professional with them. But he hasn't the brain to campaign by himself; he's just a knife in the hand of a boss, and his boss is Tolan, by the way Slats keeps turning to him. But Tolan knows even more about guns than he does about . . ."

"Damn you!" said Tolan, and charged.

The bulk of his headlong weight knocked Sleeper backwards. Tolan's driving left hand missed Sleeper's face by sheerest chance, it seemed; but the mere wind of the blow appeared to beat him towards the floor. Over his stooping body the big man stumbled. Sleeper at the same instant was rising. His hands did something strange. And Dan Tolan, lurching into the air, landed face down with a frightful crash.

Sleeper's hands dipped into Tolan's clothes; two guns flashed in his grasp as he threw them out the open door. And Tolan, rising, streaming curses and blood from a cut mouth, charged with both fists smashing. In an instant he had cornered Sleeper, measured him.

"Kill him!" screamed Slats.

The blow was a powerful straight right honestly intended to tear Sleeper's head off his shoulders; and Sleeper stood there as though overcome with terror, his hands only half raised, and open. Then, at the last instant, as the blow started whipping across, he made a frightened little gesture and whirled, as though to turn his back upon the punishment. But Tolan's arm shot harmlessly over Sleeper's shoulder, and Sleeper caught that pile-driver in a double grasp. A quick heave of Sleeper's back and shoulders converted the power of Tolan's blow into a lunge that pitched the big fellow heavily against the wall.

The shock stunned him. He dropped to his hands and knees and wavered there, dripping blood onto the floor.

The others had stopped their cheerful yelling. In a deadly silence they watched as Tolan got to his feet, staggering. With both hands he was feeling for his guns. When he found that they were gone he breathed: "Slats, he's made a fool of me. Them hands of his jar a gent silly like a mule's hoofs. Blow hell out of him, Slats!"

But Slats did not move a hand. That was very surprising to those who knew him, most of all to Dan Tolan, until his clearing eyes saw that a bright, trembling flash of a knife lay in the flat of Sleeper's hand. It was held to the side, ready for instant use; and after what he had seen, Slats would as soon have tried to dodge the stroke of a snake as the hurled point of that blade.

Sleeper was hardly breathing deep as he said: "Well, boys, why not all sit down and finish our coffee and cigarettes?"

They sat down, in silence. Dan Tolan kept licking the blood from his mouth. The coffee cup trembled in his hand.

25

The silence in which the men at the table sat was a deadly thing that grew like a sliding serpent. First they glanced at one another, and then each man looked only at his own cup of coffee or the fuming of his own cigarette, until Paley said, curiously: "What's your main business outside of taming horses and raising hell?"

He had just spoken when, outside the house, there was a faint creaking sound that made Slats jump to his feet.

"The gate to the corral!" he said.

"Inverness is leanin' against it, maybe," suggested Dan Tolan.

But the creak of the gate came again and then a horse trotted softly, passing near the house.

Without a word, the men rushed out into the moonlight and saw a tall horse striding away with a rider flattened on his back, urging him to full speed.

A keening cry came out of all those throats: "Onslow! It's Onslow that's got him!" But no man stirred to saddle a horse and pursue.

There was a good reason for that. Now that Inverness was launched beyond gunshot, like a tireless arrow he would outstride the pursuit of any mustang.

But Careless was not a mere mustang.

Sleeper cast one look at the fugitive that glimmered away into nothing through the moonlight; then he snatched up saddle and hackamore and whistled as he ran out the door. Careless came, bounding like a hunting dog when it sees the gun.

"That nag looks like he might give us a chance." Dan Tolan was inspired by the beauty of the great stallion. "Tag that gent Onslow for us, and we'll come up and smash him, Sleeper! Get your hosses, boys! On the run!"

They were already sprinting for their riding gear as Sleeper slid the saddle over the sleek back of the stallion and pulled up the cinches. It was a light saddle, made after the range pattern but without the solid mass and weight which burdens the back of a horse and is of no use except to hold the pull of the rope when a full-grown steer hits the end of the slack. The hackamore was tossed over the head of Careless; the throatlatch was not buckled until Sleeper was in the saddle, flattening himself along the neck of the horse until he had reached the strap. Then he settled himself to the work of riding a five mile race.

For the first few miles the fugitive, no matter how he trusted to the speed of his racer, would use that speed liberally to put a vital distance between himself and all possible pursuit. After that he was likely to slacken the pace of his stallion and save his strength against the challenge of a long distance.

It was probable that he had fled away on the straight line which he intended to pursue to the end of his journey; but as Sleeper strained his eyes before him, he knew that his task would be hopeless unless he actually caught sight of the other rider.

They were in the middle of a wide plateau around which the mountains reared, slashed here and there with many cañons. Those waterways, dry except in the flood-time of June when the snow dissolved suddenly along the heights, offered a hundred roads opening in any direction.

So Sleeper let Careless rush away with his huge, rolling stride, peering all the while at the trees which dotted the plain or the rolling ground before him.

At last, he saw a dim thing which did not approach him. The other tree-forms poured back to him with the gallop of Careless, but this object floated at a distance, coming only slowly, slowly towards him. As they drew together he knew that the running object was a man on horseback; he had seen the silhouette as the pair reached the top of a rise with the moonlight sky beyond them to make the outline clearer.

He looked back. Behind him there was no sight of Tolan and his three men; there was no help within reach and it would have to be a man-to-man fight if he managed to overtake Onslow.

He wished that he had had a chance to learn more about that fellow who had followed four crooks of the capacities of Tolan's gang. He wanted to hear about the man who had managed, like himself, to tame the fierce stallion and ride him away. At least, Onslow must have been a well-known enemy or his name would not have sprung instantly to the lips of the four.

One thing was certain. Such a fellow was sure to be armed to the teeth and to know how to use his weapons.

And this moonlight was so bright that it would serve almost like the sun for a good gunman. But Sleeper carried no firearms. Neither rifle nor revolver had been in hands since he had been forced into the service of Pop Lowry. The commissions of that dangerous criminal were too apt to put Sleeper in the way of taking life . . . . and he did not want to have the opportunity.

What seemed to lie before him was the task of riding up to a fighting man through some narrow, echoing cañyon and then attempting to close with him from behind.

But could Careless catch Inverness if the fugitive preferred to flee even from a single enemy? Sleeper recalled the slender black legs of the bay horse that looked like hammered iron and the length of the rein and the vast sweep of the line from the saddle to the hocks. He shook his head. Never before had he doubted the ability of Careless to run down any horse in the world—

He looked back and saw the huge, triangular head of Mount Kimbal against the moonlit sky; he looked forward and saw the smaller heights before him chopped and slashed by the ravines. Well up towards the tops of these mountains he could see the faint glow of snow under the mist which was blowing across the peaks above timberline.

Into one of those ravines the stranger entered with his horse. Sleeper followed, and after that he was under a continual strain. He had to keep his horse on the very border-line of earshot. Sight would not help him a great deal, now, because the cañyon floor twisted here and there so rapidly that the towering walls of the ravine fenced through the bright sky a narrow, winding path, a sort of cowtrail through the stars. To keep the other in view, Sleeper would have had to venture within fifty yards of him, a great part of the time.

They were climbing continually, now. Thin noises of running water underfoot mingled with the melancholy songs of waterfalls in the distance. They were up to such a height that now there was no sign of a tree except the tough lodgepole pines which are the vanguard of the Western forest, the hardy pioneers which lay down brief generations of humus before the larger trees can find rootage. Even the lodgepole pines commenced to thin out, and just above his head, Sleeper saw the bald, scalped pinnacles of the peaks, sometimes wrapped with mist, sometimes silvered over with snow and white moonlight.

Then those occasional noises ahead of Sleeper stopped. He heard no longer the clinking of the hoofs against the stones.

Sleeper allowed Careless to drift forward very quietly. The horse knew this business almost as well as his master. It was not the first time that he had been used for the stalking of danger and Careless put down his feet like a cat. Never a loose stone did he tread on. He trembled at sudden noises of wind and water on either side. He went with his ears pricked rigidly forward and his head turned just a trifle, as though to keep his eye on the trail and on his master at the same time. And, as he stole forward, his eyes blazing, his red-rimmed nostrils expanded and quivering, he seemed inspired by the eagerness of a hunting beast and an inquiring man.

The wind was against them. It blew from them up the high ravine or the next accident never could have happened. As it was, there came a sudden snort in the dimness ahead of them, and the next instant Sleeper made out a horseman mounting just before him.

"Hullo!" called the voice of the stranger.

Sleeper, silently, with one pressure of his heels, made Careless leap like a panther to the kill. He saw the flash of a drawn gun. He made out the bearded features of a man. The gun boomed almost in his face, and then he slewed himself out of the saddle and hurled himself at the other.

The impact, as he gripped the man, knocked them both headlong to the ground. Even in the air the lightning hands of Sleeper were not clenched, but he drove the edge of his palm like a blunt cleaver, again and again against the nerve center under the pit of the other man's right arm, to paralyze the man's every nerve.

Then they struck the ground, and Sleeper's head banged against a rock. The world whirled madly about him. . . .

26

He was awake. The world no longer danced in crazy waves—but as in a nightmare he could see danger without being able to do anything about it. Not a muscle of his body would respond to his will as he saw Onslow disentangle himself and rise to his feet, staggering.

The right hand with which Onslow leaned to pick up his fallen gun could not grasp the weapon, Sleeper saw. Only his left hand still functioned, but for such a fellow as Onslow that would probably be enough.

He swung about toward Sleeper, made one step toward him, and levelled the gun. This, then, was to be the last moment?

But the strangest of interruptions came. Careless, making the charge like a true warhorse, had smashed his shoulder into the beautiful bay horse and knocked him reeling. Now, recovering himself after lurching past, Careless whirled about and galloped, trumpeting with rage, straight at Inverness.

The bewilderment of Sleeper did not endure. He should have known in the first place that if two stallions caught the scent of one another they would be instantly fierce for battle. And like a pair of mountain lions, the two now flung together.

The bay was fast as a flash; so was Careless. In this mutual charge they swerved past one another, whirled, met again, rearing, and striking out with their sharp forehoofs. One stroke of those weapons would be sufficient to smash the heavy skull like paper.

Onslow, wildly shouting out, had whirled back towards the fighting horses. He fired, and Sleeper thought for a terrible moment that it was the bullet that knocked Careless to his knees. It was not the bullet, however, but a glancing blow from the hoof of Inverness that dropped the golden stallion. And the dark blood poured down Careless' head.

Inverness rushed in to finish his victory, but Careless still was full of brain power and battle wiles. He lurched to his feet and drove his head like a striking snake at Inverness' throat. His teeth glanced from the sleek of the other throat only when the blood came. In a whirling tangle the two great animals swerved about.

Sleeper, more by power of prayer than through physical strength, struggled back to his feet. Onslow was rushing this way and that trying to get in a shot that would do away with Careless without imperiling the life of Inverness. Twice he fired, but the revolver wobbled in his hand—apparently he was no two-handed gunman—and Careless went uninjured.

Drawing back a little, Careless charged Inverness, checked his attack, swerved to the side, and reared. Inverness, missing these feints, thrust in to close. But one terrible blow from a forehoof struck his side with hide-ripping force and Sleeper distinctly heard the breaking of bones.

That stroke, even though it fell upon the body, brought a human groan from the throat of the bay horse. He tried to flee, but as he turned a second hammer stroke clipped him across the head and laid him prone.

If Inverness were not dead, he would perish the next moment; and then Careless would go down under Onslow's bullets. But at this moment Sleeper found breath to cry out. It was like calling to a wild storm, but the magic of his control over the horse was so perfect that the single cry stopped Careless and sent him wincing backwards.

Onslow had turned towards the sudden voice behind him, gun in hand. A stroke from the cleaver-edge of Sleeper's palm made Onslow's left hand nerveless—and the big Colt dropped to the ground.

Even then, with his right arm quite useless and his left hand incapable, Onslow drove bravely in toward Sleeper. But he might as well have lunged at a will-o'-the-wisp. Sleeper dodged that attack and smashed Onslow once beneath the ear.

He did not even pause to watch the inert body drop to the ground. Onslow was still collapsing as Sleeper scooped the revolver from the place where it had fallen and sprang to see if life remained in Inverness.

The stallion was recovering, struggling to its knees feebly. Inverness stood at last with hanging head, blood dripping from his torn throat. He was badly hurt, to be sure, and made no movement to escape; though great

154

Careless stood on the alert, braced and ready to spring again to the battle.

Sleeper touched Inverness' torn throat. It was a mere surface wound, fortunately, and the huge swelling on the side of the horse's head was not serious, but Sleeper knew that there were cracked ribs under the lump which had risen on the side of the bay. But they would heal if the horse had rest and care.

Sleeper turned back to Onslow as the prostrate man began to struggle on the ground, returning to consciousness. Swiftly Sleeper's knowing hands wandered over the fellow, but he found no trace of another weapon except a single pocket knife of very ordinary dimensions. When he was sure of this, he stooped and helped Onslow to his feet.

Bewildered and agape, Onslow stared about him, saw Sleeper with a wild eye, and then ran toward his horse. He seemed able to see better with his hands than with his eyes, and those hands were embracing the big stallion with a trembling love.

"There's nothing to do," said Sleeper, "Those cuts are only surface slashes. They're not bleeding much now. The broken ribs are the worst part of it. Come here, Careless."

The golden stallion came to him at once, while Onslow turned slowly. He looked from Sleeper's face to the revolver in his hand; then he shook his head.

"You're with Tolan?" he asked.

"No," said Sleeper. "I'm simply taking Inverness."

He scooped from the ground a bit of soft moss and laid it over the cut on his stallion's head—but the bleeding was easing. His own head rang as though hammers were at work on anvils inside it.

"And you're the thief that Tolan expected, eh?" said Sleeper. "You're the one that he knew would be on the horse's trail? You're Onslow?"

"That's my name," said the bearded man. "But I never heard a man called a thief before because he come and took his own horse back from them that had grabbed it."

"*Your* horse!" exclaimed Sleeper.

"Sure," answered Onslow.

"I should have known," said Sleeper bitterly, "that Tolan would never be mixed up in anything but dirty work! But how do you come to own a horse like that—a thoroughbred?"

"He's no thoroughbred," said Onslow.

"He's got to be," said Sleeper, frowning as he looked over the flawless lines of the stallion.

"Mustang!" answered Onslow.

"That horse?" exclaimed Sleeper. Now he heard, far away, the clangor of many hoofs in a lower ravine, a noise that blew up for a moment on a gust of wind, and was gone. "There's Tolan now," said Sleeper.

"Yeah," answered Onslow, and said no more, but waited.

"Onslow," said Sleeper. "It's a queer thing that you've told me, but somehow I believe you. If Tolan gets up here . . ."

He shrugged his shoulders. The mist had cleared a little, though vast piles of clouds reared on either side of the brightness, towards the moon.

"They may have heard the noise of your gun," said Sleeper. "Anyway, they're coming. Onslow, suppose we try to get Inverness out of their way, broken ribs or not?"

"D'you mean that?" demanded Onslow.

"I mean it," said Sleeper. "Take his head and walk ahead of me. There, through that gap and down that ravine."

It was a narrow opening in a tall wall of the cliff at the left and through this Onslow led his stallion, looking

156

anxiously back to see how the tall bay followed; and Inverness, still with his head down, went gingerly on, stepping very short, pausing now and then as though the pain in his side were too much for him to endure.

Behind him came Sleeper and Careless—and far away the noise of hoofbeats grew constantly clearer.

27

In that narrow valley they had not gone far when they saw, at their right, a ragged cleft in the wall of the ravine that looked hardly the thickness of a man's body, but when Sleeper tried it, he found that both horse and man could pass into a cramped little gulley which, fifty feet ahead, opened out into a sort of grass-floored amphitheatre a hundred yards across, with great boulders strewn over it. The sides of this amphitheatre were so steep that hardly a fly could have climbed to the top edge.

Into that retreat they passed. As the older man pointed out, they had run to a bottle; the enemy need only discover them in it, and, from the heights around, Tolan and his crew would have them entirely at their mercy. But there was nothing else to do. They sat down in the throat of the narrow entrance, after the horses had been tethered inside the gulley. Onslow, his revolver resting on his knee, peered into the larger valley outside, and they waited for trouble.

Now and then they could hear, from the distance, the clattering of hoofs, fading out or approaching. And again a horse neighed, far off, a sound made mysterious by the flying echoes.

"What's this horse, Inverness, all about?" asked Sleeper.

Onslow said: "What are *you* about, partner? I don't make you out. You throw in with Tolan—and then you throw ag'in' him!"

"I'm only a fellow who wastes his time," answered Sleeper. "Tell me about Inverness."

"Well," said Onslow, "my father was a Scotchman who come over early and took up some mighty bare land that reminded him of the look of things around Inverness, so he called his ranch by that name. The old man made the place go, and he kept expandin' until he had a whole pile of land. It was so wild that one day a band of wild mustangs break in and run off our whole doggone cavvy. We chased those runaways, and we seen in the distance the leader, a big bay stallion, with black stockings on all four legs and a white star on his forehead. We run those hosses with relays until we got back our own, and then we legged it after that stallion, but we never could catch White Star. He could run from morning to night and laugh at us the whole time.

"We asked around, and tried to find out if any thoroughbreds had been lost in that neck of the woods." Onslow shook his head. "But there wasn't none missing. It was pretty plain that that piece of silk and iron was a mustang, though nobody never seen a mustang with the look of him, before. Well, he got in my blood. I couldn't sleep. He got between me and my chuck. I thinned out a lot, and all the time I was on the go tryin' to locate him."

Onslow leaned forward, one hand on his knee. He was frowning slightly as he went on with his story, plainly showing that it was the sole ambition in his life.

"If we couldn't catch him with hosses and a rope, I thought maybe that I could manage it by creasing him.

158

I knew that a lot of hosses had been killed, that way, because if the rifle bullet come close enough to the vertebrae to stun the hoss, it's likely to kill him, too. But I was a pretty good hand with a gun and I used to practice at snuffin' the flame of a candle about as far as I could see it good. And pretty soon I felt that I could peel an apple and core it with my .30–30. So I hit the trail, and about a month later I got a good sight of White Star. He was about half a mile away, but I wriggled and snaked along until I got close enough for a fair shot."

Onslow stopped talking for a moment. In his eyes Sleeper could see him lining the sights again for that most beautiful of all horses. Then the man went on:

"My heart was so big that my ribs were busting, but when I pulled the trigger, all the mares that were with White Star scattered, running, and the stallion dropped flat. I got up and run to him. I run as fast as I could hump it, a rope ready to tie him before he come to, but when I reached the spot, there wasn't no need of any rope to tie him. He was dead. I'd busted his neck."

"Well I took and stayed there, sleekin' him with my hand and looking at the brightness of his dead eyes, until he begun to turn cold. Then I went home.

"But I stayed sick; and the feel of his silk hide was never out of the tips of my fingers. There wasn't nothin' in life for me. There wasn't nothin' but rememberin' the finest hoss I'd ever seen—and he was dead."

Onslow's head dropped as he felt again the dejection of that day so long ago. His fingers spread in a gesture of emptiness.

"There was Judge Winthrop livin' not far away that knowed nigh everything, and I talked to him one day and he told me about mustangs that now and then turn up like freaks in the herd. You know how a mustang mostly looks—always with four good legs, but roach-backed and lumpish around the head, and ewe-necked, like as not. But the judge said that all of those mustangs come over—their ancestors, I mean—with the Spaniards. And those Spanish hosses was the Arab blood or the Barb from North Africa—the same blood that mixed with English mares to make the English thoroughbred. Hard livin' on the prairies and in the mountains made the mustangs a tough lot, all right; and it disfigured 'em a good deal. It took the shine out of them and put the devil inside in its place. But now and then one of the common mustang mares would drop a foal that was a regular throw-back to those high-headed hosses that the Spaniards brought over.

"Now, when I heard the judge talk like that, I had an idea. I'd lost White Star. I'd killed him. The only way I could bring him back to life was to make him over again, And that's what I started out to do. I hunted around through the mountains till I spotted what remained of his band, and I worked until I got some of his blood that had white blazes on the forehead, though God knows none of the hosses and none of the mares looked like a patch on White Star.

"That was when I was seventeen. I'm fifty-four now. It takes about four years to bring around a generation of hoss-flesh. And I've been workin' at that job all the time since. There's ten generations, altogether, that I kept tryin', and doggone me if ever I had a sign of luck till five years ago I bred a skinny sawbones of a stallion to a runt of a mare, and the foal she dropped had four legs under it that looked like the legs of a deer. And he had black silk stockings on all the four legs, and a white blaze, right enough, on his forehead. And when I seen him, I got my hope of what he might be.

"Well, there he is back in there. He's Inverness. I gave him that name because, about the time he was foaled, I lost pa's ranch. I'd spent my time breedin' hosses and dreamin' dreams, instead of working the herd. I didn't have wife nor child—but I had Inverness."

The pride showed in Onslow's face as he went rapidly on. The dejection seemed to have passed from his eyes. Even Sleeper began to be excited—for he was a true judge of horses, a lover of rare beauty in the animals. And anyone could see that Inverness was unusual.

"When he was six months old he could outrun the herd to water," Onslow continued proudly. "When he was a yearlin' he was faster'n a streak of lightnin'. And when he was a two-year-old, I tried him under the saddle and he went along like a dream. When I felt the wind of his gallop in my face, that was a day for me, partner! It seemed to me like fifty years of livin' meant something at last.

"Well, he was all that I had. There wasn't nothin' else. I couldn't make much money out of him here in the West, I thought, but I figgered that I could make a fortune if only I could get him into a race on an Eastern track. So I got all the money together that I could and I rode him East. Yes, sir, I rode him every step of the way because I sure never would of got the price of transportation for him along the road. And so I landed him at a race track near to New York. Well, when I showed him to a couple of gents that knew hoss flesh, they seemed kind of surprised. They put a jockey on his back—and in two seconds that jockey was ridin' air, not Inverness.

"There was where I beat myself. I'd never let a human bein' lay a strap on that colt. He loved me but he sure hated the rest of the world. I couldn't make nothin' out of him by pettin' him and introducin' him proper to the jockeys. There was one kid that spent nigh a month gettin' familiar with Inverness. No, there was nobody to ride him and I was a hundred and eighty pounds; and no hoss that ever lived could pack that much weight and win a race. There was only one man could sit the saddle on him. And that happened in a funny way, because

161

there was a stable boy that used to get pretty drunk, and while he was plastered, one day he took and climbed up on the bare back of Inverness, and sort of lay out on him, laughin', and waitin' to be bucked off. But Inverness, he never turned a hair! And later on, that feller put a saddle on him—and still Inverness took to him real kind.

"The boy begun to train him and give him regular gallops and him and Inverness got real thick. And one day there was a regular stake horse havin' a trial spin around the track, early in the morning, when Cliff— the stable boy—was ridin' Inverness, and they just hooked up and had it out with one another, and after two furlongs Inverness was about five lengths ahead, and the other jockey pulled up and said that his hoss was lame. But he wasn't lame—he was just sick, Inverness had gone away from him so fast.

"After that, Cliff, he come and told me about himself. When he was a kid, he'd been a fine jockey, but he hadn't gone straight, and he'd been ruled off the track for life for the pullin' of a hoss. He was pretty heavy, now, weighin' close to a hundred and fifty. But he says it was twelve years before that he'd been ruled off, and if he changed his name and got thinned down, he'd sure never be recognized. So I agreed with him, and he went to work. I never seen a fellow starve himself so faithful. If Cliff ever gave trouble to the world, he sure made up for it by the trouble he made for himself then. Yes, sir. He stripped the flesh off his body by ten pounds at a time and got himself down to less than a hundred and twenty.

"It was the fag end of the season when we moved off to a Florida track and Cliff registered himself under his new name. We put Inverness in a little no-account race, and the money I'd made workin' in the stables we took and bet on Inverness at ten to one. Well, sir, it was just over a mile, that race, and after half a mile was gone, Cliff had to pull his arms out to keep Inverness back. Inverness, he run the last three furlongs with his chin right on his chest and won by half a dozen lengths."

The fire was in Onslow's eyes as he visualized again that first real race. He was well warmed to his subject now and he could hardly tell his story rapidly enough. Sleeper listened patiently—not breaking in at all, as if any sign or sound from him would somehow spoil the story or cause Inverness to eventually lose out.

"It made some talk, that race, and when we entered Inverness in the Lexington Stakes some of the papers begun to write about him," Onslow continued. "There was folks said that maybe he was one of the finest hosses that had ever been kept under cover, and why had a four-year-old like that never been run before, and maybe he was not able to stand trainin'. Him with legs of steel! But they all said that no matter how good he was, he would never be able to beat the great champion, Black Velvet, or his runner-up, Galleon.

"So we put down our money. And when the Lexington Stakes was run, it was a mile and a half and the eight hosses that went out for it, they had pedigrees longer'n your arm, but not a doggone one of them had pedigrees that went back to Cortez, I reckon.

"Anyway, Galleon done the leading till they was in the home stretch, and then the champion Black Velvet, he come with a great run, and everybody yelled for him and the crowd it went crazy, because nobody noticed that outsider, Inverness, what came right up with Black Velvet into the lead.

"And a furlong from the finish, I seen Cliff let Inverness go. He come in three lengths ahead of Black Velvet, and there wasn't no sound heard except the hoofs of the hosses and some groanin' noises.

"Well, sir, we collected our money and felt pretty rich,

but then Cliff he couldn't hold himself no longer. He got drunk and started talkin'. And pretty soon he was called up by the president of the club, and they says that Cliff had been ruled off the track before and he sure was ruled off double now; and I was ruled off because I'd let Cliff ride; and Inverness was ruled off because he'd let himself be ridden.

"But there come a gent by the name of Mr. Oscar Willis and asked me what was I gunna do with Inverness and I said that I would take him out West and start breedin ag'in, and try to establish the line of Inverness as clear as a trout stream. And he says that he has a place in Kentucky, and he would be mighty pleased to own Inverness. He offered five thousand, and ten thousand, and fifteen to get Inverness for his breedin' farm, but I would'nt let him go.

"So I come on West with my hoss, and I headed across country with Inverness to go back and see could I buy a chunk of the old ranch to start the breedin' farm ag'in. The first night out, I stopped at a deserted shack, leavin' Inverness hobbled outside. And when I woke up the next mornin', Inverness, he was sure gone! I never laid eyes on him ag'in until tonight."

When he had finished his long story, Onslow packed a pipe and lighted it.

"They must've stolen the horse to send it along to this fellow Oscar Willis, in Jagtown," said Sleeper. "If he offered you fifteen thousand, he must have offered Tolan and the men behind Tolan as much as twenty-five thousand. Tolan would do ten murders for half that much coin. And you and I are nowhere near out of the woods now, Onslow."

"Anyway," said Onslow, "the dawn's comin' up, now, and we're gunna have a chance to see a few steps of our way a mite clearer, before long."

The short summer night was, in fact, already ending.

When Sleeper looked up, he could see a faint glow in the sky, with the tops of the cliffs ink-black against it. Then Onslow touched his arm.

"They're comin', partner! Look—look at the whole four of them!"

Sleeper, turning his head with a start, saw four riders moving slowly up the floor of the outer ravine, in single file.

28

All the horses drooped with weariness—the riders, however, rode erect and alert. It was plain that Dan Tolan had well-picked men with him. At the head of the procession, Dan seemed about to lead the line of riders straight on past the entrance to the amphitheatre, but when he was almost by it he turned suddenly in the saddle and looked fixedly towards the crevice in the wall of the ravine, where Onslow and Sleeper lay stretched out flat, barely venturing to peer out at this approaching danger. Then Tolan turned his horse and rode straight for the entrance to the gap!

He was within fifty feet of the crevice before he halted as suddenly as he had started, and surveyed the entrance to the chasm from head to foot, as though making sure that it could not extend to any depth into the rock. After that, with a twitch of the reins, he pulled around the head of his horse and went up the ravine.

As the other three riders followed him as before, Onslow turned to Sleeper with relief. "That's finished!" he said.

"Maybe not," said Sleeper. "We ought to get out of here. Tolan traced us this far, and he's not apt to give now!"

"How will he find us?" asked Onslow. "He sure missed us just now. He ain't a bird with wings, to hop over the mountains and look into this here bowl of ours. Partner, we found the right place; and I'm gunna stay here till I've got Inverness healed and right again."

After all, there was more of an instinctive than a reasonable objection working in Sleeper's blood. Therefore he was willing to be persuaded.

The sun had come up, actually thickening the shadows that sloped from the eastern side of the hollow, though all the heights began to blaze with light and, above them the piled clouds were burning. Then the sun was darkened. Thunder boomed from the central sky and a tremendous downpour began.

The duskiness of twilight took the place of the morning brightness. Hail rattled like a continual musketry and then the rain settled in for five tumultuous minutes. It beat up clouds of water mist from the rocks. It closed the eyes with its volleys.

The thunder shower ended as quickly as it had begun. The sun once more parted the clouds. The hollow began to flash with a great brilliance, for the sunlight was reflected across the wet walls of the amphitheatre.

Onslow and Sleeper, drenched by the water which had been bucketed over them, went into the hollow to find the horses. Careless, undepressed by the torrents, whinneyed softly to his master, but poor Inverness seemed broken in spirit. His wounds were telling on him.

They got whisps of grass, twisted them hard, and used these to brush Inverness dry. He winced when the pressure came anywhere near the swollen place on his ribs.

It had grown larger, this swelling, and it was hot to the touch.

They were still discussing the stallion when a gun spoke from the crevice which led into the hollow. The sound seemed to fly around and around through Sleeper's brain. He heard the whizzing of no bullet and yet the shock was as great as though the lead had been driven straight into his flesh.

Another rifle rang out on the height above them, and Sleeper looked up in time to see the marksman drop down behind a rock. He made out Paley's checkered shirt.

Onslow said: "They've got us, partner! They've corked the bottle and they've cracked it. We're gonna leak out and go to waste!"

It was obviously true. Sleeper, looking wildly around him, saw that the clouds were heaping higher and higher, rolled by the wind. And it seemed to him that they represented the danger which was about to overwhelm him. He had been in many perils before this time. But never had he been so completely helpless. The mouth of the crevice was stopped against their retreat. On the heights above them was at least one rifleman who needed only to take his time, moving around and around the edge of the upper bowl in complete security until he had a chance to pick off the two men, one by one, who might scuttle for a time to the refuge of one boulder and then another.

Dan Tolan's bawling voice now boomed through the valley: "Sleeper! Hey! Sleeper!" he was calling.

"Ready, Dan!" Sleeper sang out.

At this, there was a chorus of laughter from three throats. They had manned the crevice in full force and detailed only one marksman to take the heights and command the situation from the inside.

"Well, kid," said Dan Tolan, "looks like you been playin'

both ends ag'in the middle. You wanted to get Inverness for yourself, eh?"

"I seem to be here with him," said Sleeper.

"He's gunna be here without you or Onslow, before long," bawled Dan Tolan.

"Tolan," said Sleeper, "you want two horses. They'll be dead before you get the men that are with them." He added, loudly: "Onslow, put a bullet through the head of Careless to show them that we mean what we say."

He had not needed to wink at Onslow as he spoke. The latter had not stirred to draw his Colt.

But Tolan's yell broke in: "Wait a minute. Maybe we can make some kind of terms with you hombres."

"What sort of terms?" asked Sleeper.

"Talk it out! Talk it out!" pleaded Onslow, softly. "There's gunna be another cloudburst in a minute and then maybe we can do something."

"We could manage to maybe let one of you gents go free," called Tolan, "if we got the two hosses."

"Which one would you let go free?" asked Sleeper.

"We'd let you loose, kid," said Tolan instantly.

"Because poor Onslow might trail his horse and locate it as stolen goods?" asked Sleeper.

"Hold on," growled Onslow. "I ain't gonna be a spike in your coffin, Sleeper—if that's what they call you. Take your chance when it comes to you. Maybe it ain't gunna come twice!"

Sleeper, turning suddenly, looked straight into the older man's blue eyes—

"Two men can always die better than one," he said. But he added, more loudly: "How could I trust you, Tolan?"

"Come up near to the gulch here," answered Tolan, "and one of us will come out and meet you. You can have his gun for a kind of a passport through us. And once you're away—to hell with you! We'll have something to tell Pop Lowry about his Number One Boy!"

"Talk it out," urged Onslow. "There's a lot of rain hangin' up there, ready to let go all holts!"

A vast thunderhead was leaning over the hollow at the moment, increasing the height of its towers, darkening its great masses.

"Tolan, it's a hard thing for me to walk out on a poor fellow like Onslow. What have you got against him?" asked Sleeper.

"He's tied up to more money than he knows about," said Tolan. "The buzzards have gotta eat him now, Sleeper. You oughta be able to see that for youself, if you got any real sense."

One of the other men said something that Sleeper could not catch. Then Tolan called out: "We ain't gunna wait here and chatter all day. Say yes or no, Sleeper."

Sleeper looked despairingly up at the clouds which were piling in the middle sky. Then a wild impulse made him sing out: "To hell with you! I'll take my chances with Onslow."

"Are you clean crazy?" howled Tolan.

A booming of thunder broke in between, and then Sleeper heard Slats Lewis say distinctly: "Sure, all of them extra smart guys has got a screw loose somewheres."

That instant a hornet song sounded near Sleeper's head and a lead slug splattered against the face of the boulder before him. He looked vaguely at the white spot which had appeared on the weathered rock.

But, at that moment, the rain fell with a great crash that resounded through the valley like the sound of giant hands struck together.

29

Through the noise of that downpour, heavy as it was, the clang of the rifle sounded once. Then the rifleman on the height was helpless as though he were shooting down into deep water. Even Onslow had become a dim, sketchy figure before Sleeper's eyes.

But Onslow was calling: "Now, Sleeper! Let's rush 'em! Give 'em the charge, old son! Right straight for the mouth of the crevice!"

He was untethering Inverness as he spoke, and the poor, wet, beaten stallion crowded close to him like a huge child. Careless, also, was loosed in a moment. And he, too, would keep at the heels of his master.

It was obvious that this was a chance, however slender. Sleeper reached out and gripped Onslow's wet hand. Then he turned and ran lightly for the entrance to the gap.

It was like running through a dream. He could not see the walls of the amphitheatre or the ground three steps before him and he almost struck the sheer wall at the end of the hollow instead of the passageway for which he had aimed. In two quick side steps he flung into the open where he stood staring through the storm.

He saw nothing but the dull shimmering of the descending torrents of the rain; then a yellow streak flashed twice before his eyes. There was no humming of the bullets, only the booming of the reports. He dived at the figure which he made out, half risen from behind a rock.

"They're here!" yelled Joe Peek.

And then Sleeper's weight struck him. With his arm

curved over his head like the ridge of a helmet, with the hard, sharp elbow Sleeper struck his man full in the soft pit of the stomach and seemed to feel the bone of his arm jar against Peek's spinal column. The fellow went down without a sound, folding up like a jacknife over Sleeper, cushioning his headlong fall.

As he disentangled himself, Sleeper heard a gun barking from behind him. He had a glimpse of a dim figure which ran in, firing at every step. It was the gallant Onslow, coming to the attack.

Before the old fellow reached him, Onslow suddenly staggered to the side and went down. Other guns had been answering him. Through the wet came the pungent, stinging smell of the gunpowder, and the drifting smoke made the gloom even darker. In the tight space Sleeper could just make out big Dan Tolan and the tall, meagre Slats Lewis.

Only one thing was possible, and that was to strike immediately. But to rush into the blaze of those two deadly guns was like jumping into the open mouth of death. Sleeper, leaping for a jutting point of rock above his head, felt the head of a grazing bullet sear his ribs. An inch closer to his heart would have taken his life. But he swung from the rock like an acrobat from a bar—and hurled his lithe body right at the heads of the two outlaws.

Both guns blasted at his face as he shot through the air—and both bullets missed the mark. His flight from the rock had been too great a surprise for Tolan and Lewis.

Straight and true Sleeper's flinging body hit the mark. He tried to strike Slats's throat with his cleaver-edged palm, hard as a pine plank, but the fighter's long jaw, solid as stone, turned back the crashing blow and numbed Sleeper's hand.

Sleeper managed to catch Slats about the shoulders

171

and drag him down on the ground. His hands were busy as he fell. In a combat of death the hand must be as swift as the brain which manages it, and Sleeper's brain was a little quicker than the wink of lightning. So, even in falling, he struck twice, hard, against the side of Slat's neck. Those were finishing strokes. Slats lay inert on the rocks, and Sleeper whirled to grapple with Tolan.

He was too late by the fraction of a second. Tolan, heaving himself half erect after he had been knocked sprawling, hurled himself at Sleeper and caught him with one vast, mighty arm which pinioned both of Sleeper's arms to his sides.

Beaten down on his face, pinioned by the great bulk of Tolan, Sleeper turned his head and had a glimpse of the convulsed murder grin above him. He saw Tolan's hand raised with a rock clutched in the fingers. He saw the bucketing rain running on the big man's face.

And then he received, not the brain-shattering crash of that falling stone, but a soft, inert, lifeless weight. And the report of a gun boomed heavily in his ears.

Hands grasped and raised him.

"How is it, Sleeper? Did I hurt you?" shouted Onslow.

Sleeper, staggering, but erect, laughed happily.

"He's finished, Onslow. You've turned the trick!"

"Me?" said Onslow. "I was only a second chance. You're the wildcat that counted for 'em."

Blood was running down Onslow's face from a scalp wound, but he was not seriously hurt by the bullet which had floored him. He turned the heavy body of Dan Tolan on its back, but Tolan was dead. A forty-five calibre slug had drilled straight through his body. Slats Lewis lay still as a stone; Peek was beginning to groan feebly, as Sleeper and Onslow hurried out into the ravine beyond, and with the horses behind them started down the ravine.

Mr. Oscar Willis, seated on the veranda of the hotel in Jagtown, leaped suddenly to his feet and ran down to the street. A great golden stallion was walking towards the hotel, ridden by a man who led a more slenderly made bay with the fine lines of a hawk in the air.

The stranger said, as he saw Willis: "You're Oscar Willis?"

"That's my name, and that horse . . ." began Willis.

"My job is to give you the reins of Inverness," said Sleeper, "and here they are."

Willis grasped the leather with a strong hand. He was a big, fat, rosy-faced man, and now laughter began to bubble in his throat. "The money . . ." he started to say, when a bearded fellow stepped up to him and said: "Hello, Mr. Willis. You don't need to hold my hoss for me. Unless maybe you think that you're receivin' stolen goods?"

And Willis, staring at Onslow's face dropped the reins with a groan, and then, from some unannounced impulse, hoisted his fat hands in the air as though a gun had been held under his nose. The fellow on the golden stallion grinned very broadly. "It's all right, Willis," he said. "The murders you caused won't be pinned on you. But you better take a train for points East. This part of the world won't like you very long."

But Sleeper was far away from the riotous village of Jagtown when he saw, again, the tall, shambling peddler, Pop Lowry, coming down a trail. They met at an elbow turn, and Pop Lowry turned gray with rage.

"I thought you was to work for me for three months?" he exclaimed. "And here you been and give away the hoss I sent you for."

"What's the matter?" asked Sleeper. "I got the horse you sent me for, and I put his reins into Mr. Willis's hands. That's what you asked me to do."

Pop Lowry, stifled, helpless with rage, glowered for

173

an instant at his lieutenant. Then he strode on down the trail, wordless, dragging his lead mule behind him. And long after he was out of sight the light, mocking music of the bridle bells came chiming back to Sleeper's ears.

30

At the pawnbroker's window, Sleeper dismounted. He had only a few dollars in his pocket, but he had an almost childish weakness for bright things, and he could take pleasure with his eyes even when he could not buy his fancy. But on account of the peculiar slant of the sun, the only thing he could see clearly, at first, was his own image. The darkness of his skin startled him. It was no wonder that some people took him for a gypsy or an Indian. He was dressed like a gypsy vagrant, too, with a great patch on one shoulder of his shirt and one sleeve terminating in tatters at the elbow.

However, he was not one to pride himself on appearance. He stretched himself; his blue eyes closed in the completeness of his yawn. Then he pressed his face closer to the window to make out what was offered for sale.

There were trays of rings, stick pins, jeweled cuff links. There were four pairs of pearl-handled revolvers: some hatbands of Mexican wheelwork done in metal; a number of watches, silver or gold; knives; some fine lace, yellow with age; a silver tea set—who had ever drunk tea in the mid-afternoon in this part of the world?—an

174

odd bit of Mexican featherwork; spurs of plain steel, silver, or gold: and a host of odds and ends of all sorts.

The eye of Sleeper, for all his apparently lazy deliberation, moved a little more swiftly than the snapping end of a whiplash. After a glance, he had seen this host of entangled curiosities so well that he would have been able to list and describe most of them. He had settled his glance on one oddity which amused him—a key ring which was a silver snake that turned on itself in a double coil and gripped its tail in its mouth, while it stared at the world and at Sleeper with glittering little eyes of green.

Sleeper went to the door, and the great golden stallion from which he had dismounted started to follow. So he lifted a finger and stopped the horse with that small sign; then he entered.

The pawnbroker was a foreigner—he might have been anything from a German to an Armenian, and he had a divided beard that descended in two points, gray and jagged as rock. He had a yellow, wrinkled forehead, and his thick glasses made two glimmering obscurities of his eyes. When Sleeper asked to see the silver snake key ring, the bearded man took up the tray which contained it.

"How much?" asked Sleeper.

"Ten dollars," said the pawnbroker.

"Ten which?" asked Sleeper.

"With emeralds for eyes, too. But I make it seven fifty for such a young man."

Sleeper did not know jewels, but he knew men.

"I'll give you two and a half," said he.

"I sell things," answered the pawnbroker. "I can't afford to give them away."

"Good-by, brother," said Sleeper, but he had seen a shimmer of doubt in the eyes of the other and he was not surprised to be called back from the door.

"Well," said the pawnbroker, "I've only had it in my window for two or three hours; it's good luck to make a quick sale, so here you are."

And as Sleeper laid the money on the counter, he commenced to twist off the keys.

"Hold on," said Sleeper. "Let the tassels stay on it, too. They make it look better."

"You want to mix them up with your own keys?" asked the pawnbroker.

"I haven't any keys of my own," said Sleeper, laughing, and went from the pawnshop at once.

As he walked down the street, the stallion followed him, trailing a little distance to the rear, and people turned to look at the odd sight; for the horse looked fit for a king, and Sleeper was in rags. There were plenty of men in the streets of Tucker Flat, because since the bank robbery of three months ago the big mines in the Chimney Mountains north of the town had been shutting down one by one. They never had paid very much more than the cost of production, and the quarter million stolen from the Levison Bank had consisted chiefly of their deposits. Against that blow the three mines had struggled but failed to recover. And the result was that a flood of laborers was set adrift. Some of them had gone off through the mountains in a vain quest for new jobs; others loitered about Tucker Flat in the hope that something would happen to reopen the mines. That was why the sheriff had his hands full. Tucker Flat always was as hard as nails, but now it was harder still.

The streets were full, but the saloons were empty, as Sleeper soon observed when he went into one for a glass of beer. He sat at the darkest corner table, nursing the drink and his gloomy thoughts. Pop Lowry had appointed this town and that evening as the moment for their meeting, and only the devil that lived in the brain of the pseudopeddler could tell what new and dangerous task Lowry would name for Sleeper.

He had been an hour in the shadows, staring at his thoughts, before the double swing doors of the saloon were pushed open by a man who looked over the interior with a quick eye, then muttered: "Let's try the redeye in here, old son."

With a companion, he sauntered toward the bar; and Sleeper was at once completely awake. For that exploring glance which the stranger had cast around the room had not been merely to survey the saloon; it had been in quest of a face and when his eye had lighted on Sleeper, he had come in at once.

But what could Sleeper be to him?

Sleeper had never seen him before. In the great spaces of his memory, where faces appeared more thickly than whirling leaves, never once had he laid eyes on either of the pair. The first man was tall, meager, with a crooked neck and a projecting Adam's apple. The skin was fitted tightly over the bones of his face; his hair was blond, his eyebrows very white, and his skin sun-blackened. It was altogether a face that would not be forgotten easily. The second fellow was an opposite type, fat, dark, with immense power swelling the shoulders and sleeves of his shirt.

The two looked perfectly the parts of cowpunchers; certainly they had spent their lives in the open: and there was nothing to catch the eyes about them as extraordinary except that both wore their guns well down the thigh, so that the handles of them were conveniently in grasp of the finger tips.

Having spent half a second glancing at them, Sleeper spent the next moments in carefully analyzing the two. Certainly he never had seen their faces. He never had heard their names—from their talk he learned that the tall fellow was Tim and the shorter man was called "Buzz." They looked the part of cowpunchers, perfectly, except that the palms of their hands did not seem to be thickened or calloused.

What could they want with Sleeper unless they had been sent in to the town of Tucker Flat in order to locate Sleeper and relay to him orders from Pop Lowry?

Several more men came into the saloon. But it was apparent that they had nothing to do with the first couple. However, a few moments later both Buzz and Tim were seated at a table with two more. By the very way that tall Tim shuffled the cards, it was clear to Sleeper that these fellows probably had easier ways of making money than working for it.

Hands uncalloused; guns worn efficiently though uncomfortably low; these were small indications, but they were enough to make Sleeper suspicious. The two looked to him more and more like a couple of Lowry's lawbreakers.

"How about you, stranger?" said Tim, nodding at Sleeper. "Make a fifth at poker?"

"I've only got a few bucks on me," said Sleeper. "But I'll sit in if you want."

He could have sworn that this game had been arranged by Tim and Buzz solely for the purpose of drawing him into it. And yet everything had been done very naturally.

He remained out for the first three hands; then on three queens he pulled in a jack pot. Half an hour later he was betting his last penny. He lost it at once.

"You got a nice spot of bad luck," said Buzz Mahoney, who was mixing the cards at the moment. "But stick with the game. If you're busted, we'll lend you something."

"I've got nothing worth a loan," said Sleeper.

"Haven't you got a gun tucked away, somewhere?"

"No. No gun."

And he saw a thin gleam of wonder and satisfaction commingled in the eyes of Tim Riley.

"Empty out your pockets," said Tim. "Maybe you've got a picture of your best girl. I'll lend you something on that."

He laughed as he spoke. They all laughed. And Sleeper obediently put the contents of his pockets on the table, a jumble of odds and ends.

"All right," said Tim at once. "Lend you ten bucks on that, brother."

Ten dollars? The whole lot was not worth five, new. But Sleeper accepted the money. He accepted and lost it all by an apparently foolish bet in the next hand.

But he wanted to test the stranger at once.

"I'm through, boys," he said, and pushed back his chair.

He was eager to see if they would still persuade him to remain in the game. But not a word was said, except that Buzz Mahoney muttered: "Your bad luck is a regular long streak, today. Sorry to lose you, kid."

Sleeper laughed a little, pushing in his cards with a hand that lingered on them for just an instant.

In that moment he had found what he expected—a little, almost microscopic smudge which was not quite true to the regular pattern on the backs of the cards. It was a tiny thing, but the eye of Sleeper was a little sharper than that of a hawk which turns its head in the middle sky and sees in the dim forest of the grass below the scamper of a little field mouse.

The cards were marked. Mahoney or Tim Riley had done that. They were marked for the distinct purpose of beating Sleeper, for the definite end of getting away something that had been in his possession.

What was it that they had wanted so much? What was it that had brought them on his trail?

31

It was pitch dark when Pop Lowry reached the deserted shack outside the town of Tucker Flat. He whistled once and again, and when he received no answer, he began to curse heavily. In the darkness, with the swift surety of long practice, he stripped the packs from the mules, hobbled and side-lined them; and presently they were sucking up water noisily at the little rivulet which crossed the clearing.

The peddler, in the meantime, had kindled a small fire in the open fireplace which stood before the shack and he soon had the flames rising, as he laid out his cooking pans and provisions. This light struck upward only on his long jaw and heavy nose, merely glinting across the baldness of his head and the silver pockmarks which were littered over his features. When he turned, reaching here or there with his long arms, the huge, deformed bunch behind his shoulders loomed. It was rather a camel's hump of strength than a deformity of the spine.

Bacon began to hiss in the pan. Coffee bubbled in the pot. Potatoes were browning in the coals beside the fire. Soft pone steamed in its baking pan; and now the peddler set out a tin of plum jam and prepared to begin his feast.

It was at this moment that he heard a yawn, or what seemed a yawn, on the farther side of the clearing.

The big hands of the peddler instantly were holding a shotgun in readiness. Peering through the shadows, on the very margin of his firelight he made out a dim patch of gold; then the glow of big eyes; and at last he was aware of a big horse lying motionless on the ground while close to him, his head and shoulders comfortably pillowed on a hummock, appeared Sleeper.

"Sleeper!" yelled the peddler. "You been here all the time? Didn't you hear me whistle?"

"Why should I show up before the eating time?" asked Sleeper.

He stood up and stretched himself. The stallion began to rise, also, but a gesture from the master made it sink to the ground again.

"I dunno why I should feed a gent too lazy to help me take off those packs and cook the meal." growled Pop Lowry. And he thrust out his jaw in an excess of malice.

"You want to feed me because you always feed the hungry," said Sleeper. "Because the bigness of old Pop's heart is one of the things that every one talks about. A rough diamond, but a heart of gold. A————"

"The devil with the people and you, too," said Pop.

He looked on gloomily while Sleeper, uninvited, helped himself to food and commenced to eat.

"Nothing but brown sugar for this coffee?" demanded Sleeper.

"It's too good for you, even that way," answered Pop. "What makes you so hungry?"

"Because I didn't eat since noon."

"Why not? There's all the food in the world in Tucker Flat."

"Broke," said Sleeper.

"Broke? How can you be broke when I gave you fifteen hundred dollars two weeks ago?" shouted Pop.

"Well," said Sleeper, "the fact is that faro parted me from five hundred."

"Faro? You fool!" said Pop. "But that still left a whole thousand—and from the looks of you, you didn't spend anything on clothes."

"I ran into Jeff Beacon, and old Jeff was flat."

"How much did you give him?"

"I don't know. I gave him the roll, and he took a part of it."

"You don't know how much?"

"I forgot to count it, afterwards."

"Are you clean crazy, Sleeper?"

"Jeff needed money worse than I did. A man with a family to take care of needs a lot of money, Pop."

"Still, that left you several hundred. What happened to it?"

"I met Steve Walters when he was feeling lucky and I staked him for poker."

"What did his luck turn into?"

"Wonderful. Pop. He piled up nearly two thousand in an hour."

"Where was your share of it?"

"Why, Steve hit three bad hands and plunged, and he was taken to the cleaners. So I gave him something to eat on and rode away."

Sleeper added: "And when today came along, somehow I had only a few dollars in my pocket."

"I'd rather pour water on the desert than put money in your pocket!" shouted Pop Lowry. "It ain't human, the way you throw it away."

He continued to glare for a moment, and growl. He was still shaking his head as he commenced champing his food.

"You didn't even have the price of a meal?" he demanded at last.

"That's quite a story."

"I don't want to hear it," snapped Pop Lowry. "I've got a job for you."

"I've just finished a job for you," said Sleeper.

"What of it?" demanded Pop Lowry. "You signed up to do what I pleased for three months, didn't you?"

"I did," sighed Sleeper. He thought regretfully of the impulse that had led him into putting himself at the beck and call of this old vulture. But his word had been given.

"And there's more than two months of that time left, ain't there?"

"I suppose so."

"Then listen to me, while I tell you what I want you to do."

"Wait till you hear my story."

"Rats with your story. I don't want to hear it."

"Oh, you'll want to hear it all right."

"What makes you think so?" asked the peddler.

"Because you like one thing even more than money."

"What do I like more?"

"Trouble," said Sleeper. "You love it like the rat that you are."

In fact, as the peddler thrust out his jaw and wrinkled his eyes he looked very like a vast rodent.

He overlooked the insult to ask: "What sort of trouble?"

"Something queer. I told you I was broke today. That's because I lost my last few dollars playing poker. I played the poker because I *wanted* to lose."

"Wanted to?" echoed Pop Lowry. "That's too crazy even for you. I don't believe it."

"I'll tell you how it was. I was sitting with a glass of beer when two hombres walked into the saloon; by the look they gave me, I knew they were on my trail: and I wondered why, because I'd never seen them before. I let them get me into a poker game and take my cash. I knew that wasn't what they wanted. When I was frozen out, they were keen to lend me a stake and got me to empty my pockets on the table. I put a handful of junk on the table, then they loaned me ten dollars, and I let that go in the next hand. They didn't offer to stake me again. They wanted something that was in my pockets. When they got that, they were satisfied. Now, then, what was it that they were after?"

"What did they look like?" asked Pop Lowry.

"Anything up to murder," said Sleeper promptly.

"What was the stuff you put on the table?"

"Half a pack of wheat-straw papers, a full sack of tobacco, a penknife with one blade broken, a twist of twine, sulphur matches, a leather wallet with nothing in it except a letter from a girl, a key ring and some keys, a handkerchief, a pocket comb in a leather case, a stub of a pencil. That was all."

"The letter from the girl. What girl?" asked Lowry.

"None of your business," said Sleeper.

"It may have been *their* business, though."

"Not likely. Her name wasn't signed to the letter, any-way. She didn't say anything except talk about the weather. Nobody could have made anything of that letter."

"Any marks on the wallet?"

"None that mattered, so far as I know."

"I've seen you write notes on cigarette papers."

"No notes on those."

"What were you doing with a key ring and keys? You don't own anything with locks on it."

"Caught my eye in the pawnshop to-day. Little silver snake with green eyes."

"Anything queer about that snake?"

"Good Mexican work. That's all."

"The letter's the answer," said Pop Lowry. "There was something in that letter."

"They're welcome to it."

"Or in the keys. What sort of keys?"

"Three for padlocks, two regular door keys, some-thing that looked like a skeleton, and a little flat key of white metal."

"Any marks on those keys?"

"Only on the little one. The number on it was 1265."

184

"You've got an eye," said Pop Lowry. "When I think what an eye and a brain and a hand you've got, it sort of makes me sick. Nothin' in the world that you couldn't do if you weren't so dog-gone honest."

Sleeper did not answer. He was brooding, and now he said: "Could it have been the keys? I didn't think of that!"

Then he added: "It *was* the keys!"

"How d'you know?" asked Pop.

"I remember now that when I bought them, the pawn-broker said that he had just put the ring out for sale a couple of hours before."

"Ha!" grunted Pop. "You mean that the two gents had gone back to the pawnshop to redeem the key ring?"

"Why not? Maybe they'd come a long way to redeem that key ring. Maybe the time was up yesterday. They found the thing gone; they got my description; they trailed me; they worked the stuff out of my pockets onto the table; and there you are! Pop, they were headed for some sort of dirty work—something big."

Pop Lowry began to sweat. He forgot to drink his coffee.

"We'll forget the other job I was going to give you," he said. "Maybe there ain't a bean in this, but we'll run it down."

"I knew you'd smell the poison in the air and like it," said Sleeper, grinning.

"What would put you on their trail? What would the number on that little key mean?"

"Hotel room? No, it wasn't big enough for that. It couldn't mean anything—in this part of the world—except a post-office box. No other lock would be shallow enough for it to fit."

"There's an idea!" exclaimed Pop Lowry. "That's a big number—1265. Take a big town to have that many post-office boxes."

"Weldon is the only town big enough for that—the

185

only town inside of three hundred miles."

"That pair is traveling for Weldon," agreed Lowry. "They wanted that bunch of keys. Get 'em, Sleeper! That's your job. Just get those keys and find out what they're to open. And start now!"

32

Buzz Mahoney, opening the door of his room at the hotel in Tucker Flat, lighted a match to ignite the lamp on the center table. Then he heard a whisper behind him and tried to turn around, but a blow landed accurately at the base of his skull and dropped him down a well of darkness. Sleeper, leaning over him, unhurried, lighted another match, and fumbling through the pockets, found almost at once the silver snake key ring. Then he descended to the street, using a back window instead of the lobby and the front door. Before he had gone half a block, he heard stamping and shouting in the hotel, and knew that his victim had recovered and was trying to discover the source of his fall.

Sleeper, pausing near the first streak of lamplight that shone through a window, examined the keys with a swift glance.

There had been seven keys before; there were only six, now. That was what sent Sleeper swiftly around the corner to the place where Pop Lowry waited for him.

"I've got them," he said. "but the one for the post-office box is gone. Mahoney had the rest: but Tim Riley is gone with the little key."

"There's something in that post-office box," answered Pop. "Go and get it."

"He's got a good head start," answered Sleeper.

"He's got a good start, but you've got your horse, and if Careless can't make up the lost ground, nothing can. Ride for Weldon and try to catch Tim Riley on the way. I'm heading straight on for Weldon, myself. I'll get there sometime tomorrow. Quit the trails and head straight for Weldon Pass. You'll catch your bird there."

Sleeper sat on his heels and closed his eyes. He was seeing in his mind all the details of the ground over which he would have to travel, if he wished to take a short cut to Weldon Pass. Then he stood up, nodded, stretched again.

"I'll run along," he said.

"Have another spot of money?" asked the peddler.

He took out fifty dollars, counted it with a grudging hand from his wallet, and passed it to Sleeper, who received it without thanks.

"How long before somebody cuts your gizzard open to get your money, Pop?" he asked.

"That's what salts the meat and makes the game worth while," said Pop Lowry. "Never knowing whether I'm gonna wake up when I go to sleep at night."

"How many murders do you dream about, Pop?" pursued Sleeper casually.

"I got enough people in my dreams," said Pop Lowry, grinning. "And some of 'em keep on talking after I know they're dead. But my conscience don't bother me none. I ain't such a fool, Sleeper."

Sleeper turned on his heel without answer or farewell. Five minutes later he was traveling toward Weldon Pass on the back of the stallion.

If Tim Riley had in fact started so long ahead of him

toward the town of Weldon, it would take brisk travel to catch him in the narrow throat of the Pass, so Sleeper laid out an air line and traveled it as straight as a bird. There were ups and downs which ordinary men on ordinary horses never would have attempted. Sleeper was on his feet half the time; climbing rugged slopes up which the stallion followed him like a great cat; or again Sleeper worked his way down some perilous steep with the golden horse scampering and sliding to the rear, always with his nose close to the ground to study the exact places where his master had stepped. For the man knew exactly what the horse could do, and never took him over places too slippery or too abrupt for him to cover. In this work they gave the impression of two friends struggling toward a common end, rather than of master and servant.

So they came out on a height above Weldon Pass, and looking down it, Sleeper saw the moon break through clouds and gild the Pass with light. It was a wild place, with scatterings of hardy brush here and there, even an occasional tree, but on the whole it looked like a junk heap of stone with a course kicked through the center of it. Rain had been falling recently. The whole Pass was bright with water, and it was against the thin gleam of this background that Sleeper saw the small shadow of the other rider coming toward him. He went down the last abrupt slope at once to intercept the course of the other rider.

He was hardly at the bottom before he could hear the faint clinking sounds made by the hoofs of the approaching horse. A whisper made the stallion sink from view behind some small boulders. Sleeper himself ran up to the top of a boulder half the size of a house and crouched there. He could see the stranger coming, the head of the horse nodding up and down in the pale moonlight. Sleeper tied a bandanna around the lower part of his face.

Ten steps from Sleeper's waiting place, he made sure that it was tall Tim Riley in person: for there Riley stopped his horse and let it drink from a little freshet that ran across the narrow floor of the ravine. It was a magnificent horse that he rode—over sixteen hands, sloping shoulders, high withers, big bones, well-let-down hocks, and flat knees; a horse too good for a working cowpuncher to have, thought Sleeper. And his last doubt about the character of Tim Riley disappeared. The man was a crooked card player with a crooked companion; he was probably a criminal in other ways, as well. Men are not apt to make honest journeys through the middle of the night and over places as wild as the Weldon Pass.

When the horse had finished drinking, Riley rode on again. He was passing the boulder that sheltered Sleeper when his mount stopped suddenly and threw up its head with a snort. Riley, with the speed of an automatic reaction, snatched out a gun. There was a well-oiled ease in the movement, a professional touch of grace that did not escape the eye of Sleeper. He could only take his man half by surprise, now, but he rose from behind his rampart of rock and leaped, headlong.

He sprang from behind, yet the flying shadow of danger seemed to pass over the brain of Riley. He jerked his head and gun around while Sleeper was still in the air; then Sleeper struck him with the full lunging weight of his body, and they rolled together from the back of the horse.

The gun had exploded once while they were in the air; Sleeper remained unscathed; and now he found himself fighting for his life against an enemy as strong and swift and fierce as a mountain lion.

A hundred times Sleeper had fought with his hands, but always victory had been easy. The ancient science of jujutsu, which he had spent patient years learning, gave him a vast advantage in spite of his slender bulk. He had struggled with great two hundred pounders who were hardened fighting men, but always it was like the battle between the meager wasp and the huge, powerful tarantula. The spider fights with blind strength, laying hold with its steel shears wherever it can; the wasp drives its poisoned sting at the nerve centers.

And that is the art of jujutsu. At the pits of the arms or the side of the neck or the back, or inside the legs or in the pit of the stomach, there are places where the great nerves come close to the surface, vulnerable to a hard pressure or a sharp blow. And Sleeper knew those spots as an anatomist might know them. Men who fought him were rarely hurt unless they hurled their own weight at him too blindly, for half the great art of jujutsu lies in using the strength of the antagonist against him. Usually the victim of Sleeper recovered as from a trance, with certain vaguely tingling pains still coursing through parts of his body. But not a bone would be broken, and the bruises were few.

He tried all his art now, and he found that art checked and baffled at every turn. Tall and spare of body, Tim Riley looked almost fragile, but from the first touch Sleeper found him a creature of whalebone and Indian rubber. Every fiber of Riley's body was a strong wire, and in addition he was an expert wrestler. Before they had rolled twice on the ground, Sleeper was struggling desperately in the defense.

Then the arm of Riley caught him with a frightful strangle hold that threatened to break his neck before it choked him. Suddenly Sleeper lay still.

Tim Riley seemed to sense surrender in this yielding, this sudden pulpiness of body and muscle. Instead of offering quarter, Riley began to snarl like a dog that has sunk its teeth in a death grip. He kept jerking the crook of his arm deeper and deeper into the throat of Sleeper, who lay inert, face down. Flames and smoke seemed to shoot upward through Sleeper's brain, but in that instant of relaxation he had gathered his strength and decided on his counterstroke.

He twisted his right leg outside that of his enemy, raised the foot until with his heel he located the knee of Riley, then kicked the sharp heel heavily against the inside of the joint.

Tim Riley yelled with agony. The blow fell again, and he twisted his body frantically away from the torture. That movement gave Sleeper his chance and with the sharp edge of his palm, hardened almost like wood by long practice in the trick, he struck the upper arm of Riley.

It loosened its grip like a numb, dead thing. With his other arm Riley tried to get the same fatal hold, but Sleeper had twisted like a writhing snake. He struck again with the edge of the palm, and the blow fell like the stroke of a blunt cleaver across the million nerves that run up the side of the neck. The head of Riley fell over as though an ax had struck deep. He lay not motionless but vaguely stirring, making a groaning, wordless complaint.

Sleeper, in a moment, had trussed him like a bird for market. Still the wits had not fully returned to Riley as Sleeper rifled his pockets. But he found not a sign of the little flat white key which had the number 1265 stamped upon it.

He crumpled the clothes of the man, feeling that such a small object might have been hidden in a seam; then he pulled off the boots of Riley and when he took out the first insole, he found what he wanted. The little key flashed like an eye in the moonlight: then he dropped it into his pocket.

The voice of Tim Riley pleaded from the ground: "You ain't gonna leave me here, brother, are you? And what on earth did you use to hit me? Where did you have it, up your sleeve?"

Sleeper leaned and looked into the lean, hard face of the other. Then he muttered: "You'll be all right. People will be riding through the Pass in the early morning. So long, partner."

Then he took the horse of Riley by the reins and led it away among the rocks toward the place where he had left Careless, the stallion.

33

Neither on the streets of Weldon nor in the post office itself did people pay much attention to Sleeper because the Weldon newspaper had published an extra which told that the body of Joe Mendoza, the escaped fugitive from the state prison, had been found. That news was of sufficient importance to occupy all eyes with reading and all tongues with talk; but all it meant to Sleeper was the cover under which he could approach his work.

He went straight into the post office and found there what he had expected in a town of the size of Weldon —a whole wall filled by the little mail boxes, each with a glass insert in the door so that it could be seen if mail were waiting inside.

And in the right-hand corner, shoulder-high, appeared No. 1265. Inside it, he could see a single thin envelope.

The key fitted at once; the little bolt of the lock slipped with a click, and the door opened. Sleeper took out the envelope and slammed the small door so that the spring lock engaged.

On the envelope was written: "Mr. Oliver Badget, Box 1265, Weldon." And in the upper left-hand corner: "To be delivered only to Oliver Badget in person."

The camping places of the peddler in his tours through the mountains were perfectly known to Sleeper; therefore he was waiting in a wooded hollow just outside of Weldon when Pop Lowry shambled into the glade late that afternoon.

Pop Lowry shouted an excited greeting, but Sleeper remained flat on his back, his hands cupped under his head while he stared up through the green gloom of a pine tree at the little splashes of blue heaven above. The sun in slanted patches warmed his body.

But the peddler, not waiting to pull the pack saddles off his tired mules, stood over Sleeper and stared critically down at him.

"That gent Riley was a tough hombre, eh? Too tough for you, Sleeper?" he asked.

"I got the key from him," said Sleeper. "There was a box numbered 1265 at the post office, and this was what was inside."

He fished the envelope from his pocket and tossed it into the air. The big hand of the peddler darted out and caught the prize. Jerking out the fold of paper which it contained, Pop Lowry stared at a singular pattern; there was not a written word on the soiled sheet; there was only a queer jumble of dots, triangles, and one wavering, crooked line that ran across the paper from one corner to the other.

Beside one bend of the wavering line appeared a cross.

"This here is the spot," argued the peddler.

"The cross is the spot," agreed Sleeper. "And a lot that means?"

"The triangles are trees," said Pop.

"Or mountains," answered Sleeper.

"The dots—what would they be, kid?"

"How do I know? Cactus—rocks—I don't know."

"This crooked line is a road, Sleeper."

"Or a valley, or a ravine."

"It's hell!" said Lowry.

He stared at Sleeper, who remained motionless. The wind ruffled his black hair; the blue of his eyes was as still and peaceful as the sky above them. Pop Lowry cursed again and then sat down, cross-legged.

"Put your brain on this here, Sleeper," he said. "Two brains are better than one."

"I've put my brain on it, but you can see for yourself that we'll never make anything out of it."

"Why not?"

"Well, it's simply a chart to stir up the memory of Oliver Badget. Oliver is the boy who knows what those marks mean. Call it a road—that crooked line. Well, at the seventh bend from the lower corner of the page, there, along that road, there's something planted. Oliver wants to be able to find it. But where does the road begin? Where does he begin to count the bends?"

"From Weldon," suggested the peddler.

"Yes. Or from a bridge, or a clump of trees, or something like that. And there's twenty roads or trails leading into Weldon."

Pop Lowry groaned.

He took out a plug of chewing tobacco, clamped his teeth into a corner of it, and bit off a liberal quid with a single powerful closing of his jaws. He began to masticate the tobacco slowly.

"A gent with something on hand wants to put it away," he said, thinking aloud. "He takes and hides it. He hides it in a place so doggone mixed up that even he can't be sure that he'll remember. So he leaves a chart. Where's he going to hide the *chart*, though?"

"Where nobody would ever think of looking," agreed Sleeper. "He rents a post-office box and puts the chart in an envelope addressed to himself. Nobody else could get that envelope because nobody else has the key, and nobody could call for mail in Badget's name and get the envelope, either. Because that letter would have to be signed for in Badget's signature before the clerk would turn the thing over. But now that he's got the chart hidden, all he has to do is to hide the key. And where would he hide the key? Well, in a place just as public as the post-office box, where everybody could see it. So he hocks that key ring and all the keys on it at a pawnshop."

Lowry sighed.

"Nobody would go to all of this trouble, Sleeper," he commented, "unless what was hidden out was a dog-gone big pile."

"Nobody would," agreed Sleeper.

"And now Mr. Badget turns up and tries to get his key and finds that his time has just run out. He hurries like the devil to get to that key in time, but he's too late. Sleeper has the key. He gets it away from Sleeper. . . . Why, that all sounds dog-gone reasonable and logical."

"Badget isn't another name for Riley or for Mahoney," declared Sleeper.

"Why not?"

"Well, Badget himself could go to the post office without the key and get the letter any time by signing for it."

"True," agreed Lowry.

Then he added, after a moment of thought: "Badget couldn't come himself. He had to send friends to make sure that that key didn't get into the wrong hands. He sent friends to maybe just pay the interest due on the pawnbroker's loan and renew it, and pay for the post-office box. Why didn't Badget come himself? Sick? In jail?"

"Or dead," said Sleeper.

"Sleeper, there's something important hidden out where that cross is marked."

"We'll never find it without a key to the chart," said Sleeper. "It's a good little map, all right, but unless we know what part of the country to fit it to, we'll never locate what's under the cross. It may be a district five hundred miles from here, for all we know."

"What'll we do?" asked Pop Lowry.

"Wait, Pop. That's the only good thing that we can do."

"What good will waiting do?"

"The postmaster has a master key for all of those boxes. Well, the postmaster is going to lose that key today or tomorrow. And right afterwards, Box 1265 is going to be opened."

"There won't be anything in it," protested Lowry. "Whatcha mean, Sleeper?"

"You can copy the chart, and then I'll put the original back in the post-office box."

"What happens then? You mean that Riley and Mahoney come along, rob the postmaster of the master key, get the chart, and then start out on the trail with us behind them?"

"With *me* behind them," corrected Sleeper. "I don't need you."

The big peddler swore.

"Yeah," he said, "you can disappear like a sand flea and turn up like a wild cat whenever you want to. You'll be able to trail 'em, all right."

Sleeper sighed.

"Copy the chart," he said. "I'm going to sleep. Because after I take that envelope back to the post office, I've got to find a place and stay awake day and night to see who goes into that building, and who comes out again."

Lowry, without a word of answer, sat down to his drawing.

34

There was a three-story hotel opposite the post office, and here Sleeper lay at a window night and day for four long days. They were hot, windless days, and he hardly closed his eyes for more than a half hour at a time, but the keenness of his attention never diminished. Over the low shoulders of the post office, from his place of vantage, he could look all around the environs of the building he spied upon. The nights were clear, with moonlight; the days were the more difficult.

Because he could not tell when Riley or Mahoney would appear in one of the sudden swirls of people who slipped suddenly through the swing doors of the building, disappeared, and came out again a few moments later.

It was quite possible that they would attempt to disguise themselves. But even then he would have more than a good chance of identifying them. He had learned long ago to look not only at the face of a man but also at the shape of his head, the angle of nose and forehead, and particularly at any strangeness of contour in the ear. A man may become either thin or fat, but his height is not altered. And the general outline of the head and shoulders, whether the man comes toward the eye or goes from it, may often be recognized.

Even so, hawk-eyed as he was, it would be fumbling in the dark—and like a patient fisher he remained waiting. Agonies of impatience he hid away behind a smile.

One cause of his impatience was his desire to finish up the job for Lowry. Pop had helped him in his great need but had expected a three months' servitude in exchange. Sleeper loved danger, and Pop could supply it, but it was unsavory, unclean, and Sleeper liked things as shining clear as the coat of the stallion Careless. But his code made him live up to his given word. What he would do to Pop when his term of service was up put the only good taste in his mouth in many a day.

It was on the fourth day that tall Pop Lowry stalked into the room and pushed his dusty hat back on his head. The hot reek of the outdoors entered with him.

He said: "Oliver Badget was Joe Mendoza. I just seen a bit of Mendoza. I just seen a bit of Mendoza's handwriting, so I know. Buzz Mahoney and Tim Riley were the best friends of Joe. Mendoza is dead. Buzz and Tim are carryin' on where Mendoza left off. That means they're starting something big. So big, that Mendoza risked his neck to get out of prison. He must 'a' met those two hombres. Before he died, he told them things. And it's my idea, Sleeper, that what that chart tells is the location of the cache where Mendoza put away the whole savin's of his life."

The teeth of Lowry clicked together. His eyes grew green with bright greed. "And Mendoza never spent nothin'. He never did nothin' but save," he added. "Sleeper, I've got three of my best men, and they're gonna ride with you when you start the game."

"I work a lone hand or I don't work at all," said Sleeper dreamily, as he lay stretched on his bed, peering steadily out the window.

"Damn it," growled Lowry, "if you try to handle the two of 'em, they'll sure bust you full of lead. Mendoza never had nothin' to do with gents that wasn't murderers. Those are two gunmen, Sleeper, and when you handled 'em before, you was dealin' with rattlers without knowin' it."

"I'll handle 'em alone or not at all," said Sleeper in the same voice.

"Sleeper—you'll carry a gun, then, won't you?"

Sleeper shook his head. "Any fool can carry a gun," he answered. "The fun of the game is handling fire with your bare hands."

There was a muffled, snarling sound from Pop Lowry. Then he strode from the room without another word.

And five minutes later Sleeper shuddered. For a man with a long linen duster on had just stepped through the front door of the post office. The duster covered him very efficiently, but a certain weight about the shoulders, a certain sense of power in the arms was not lost on Sleeper.

He was off his bed, down the stairs, and instantly in the stable behind the hotel. A moment later he had jerked the saddle on the back of the stallion and snapped the bridle over his head. Then he hurried down the alley and crossed into the vacant lot beside the hotel where a clump of tall shrubs covered him. He could see without being seen.

And he had hardly taken his post before the man in the linen duster came out from the post office again, paused to yawn widely, glanced up and down the street with quick eyes, and turned the corner.

Sleeper, running to the same corner, had a glimpse of two men swinging on the backs of two fine horses. At once the pair swung away at a rapid canter.

They left Weldon, headed north for five miles, swung sharply to the west, then went straight south through the mountains. For two days, Sleeper shivered in the wet winds and the whipping rains of the high ravines, following his quarry.

It was close work, dangerous work. Sometimes in a naked valley he had to let the pair get clear out of sight before he ventured to take the trail again. Once, coming through a dense fog which was simply a cloud entangled in the heights, he came suddenly around a rock face to face with a starry light. And through the mist, not five steps away, he heard the loud voice of Buzz Mahoney yell out: "Who's there? What's that?"

"A mountain sheep, you fool," suggested Tim Riley.

Six days out of Weldon, Sleeper was riding anxiously through a ravine that was cluttered with such a litter of rocks that danger might have hidden there in the form of whole regiments. It was only the hair-trigger sensitiveness of the nose of the stallion that detected trouble ahead.

He stopped, jerked up his head, and the next instant Sleeper saw the wavering of sunlight on a bit of steel, the blue brightness of a leveled gun.

He whirled Careless away. Two rifles barked, sent long, clanging echoes down the ravine, and Sleeper swayed slowly out from the saddle, dropped, and hung head-down with trailing arms, his right leg hooked over the saddle as though caught in the stirrup leather and so, precariously, supported.

The rifles spoke no more.

Instead, two riders began to clatter furiously in pursuit. A good mile they rushed their swift horses along, but Careless, with his master still hanging at his side, widened the distance of his lead with every stride and finally was lost to view among the sea of boulders.

After that, the noise of the pursuit no longer beat through the ravine; and Sleeper pulled himself back into the saddle. His leg ached as though the bone had been broken: his head spun; but there was no real harm done by his maneuver.

He turned again on the trail. All that Pop Lowry had told him, all that he could have guessed, was re-enforced doubly now. For when men would not delay to capture such a horse as Careless when the rider was apparently wounded to death, it was sure proof that Mahoney and Riley were bound toward a great goal.

They went on securely, now, but steadily. They cleft

through the mountains, following the high Lister Pass, and then they dipped down along the side of the range into the terrible sun mist and dusty glare of Alkali Flat.

Imagine a bowl a hundred miles across, rimmed with cool blue distance on either side but paved with white heat and the welter and dance of the reflected sun. That was Alkali Flat.

Sleeper, looking from the rim of the terrible depression, groaned softly. He glanced up and saw three soaring buzzards come over the head of the mountain, turn, and sweep with untroubled wings back the way they had come.

Even at that height, they seemed to dread the pungent heat that poured up from the vast hollow.

Sleeper, sitting in the shadow of a rock, sat down to think. He could find no resource in his mind. There was no way in which he could travel out into the desert.

Whoever had chosen to hide a treasure in the midst of such an ocean of despair had chosen well.

In the middle of the day, a man needed three pints of water an hour.

A fellow whose canteen went dry in the middle of that hell would be mad with thirst by the time he had walked fifteen miles, at the most.

They went mad and died—every man the same way. The first act was to tear off the shirt. The second was to commence digging with bare hands in the sand and the rocks. They would be found that way afterward, the nails broken from their fingers, the flesh tattered, the very bones at the tips of the fingers splintered by the frightful, blind efforts of the dying men.

Sleeper, remembering one dreadful picture he had seen, slowly ran the pink tip of his tongue across his lips and sat up to breathe more easily.

He had a canteen that would hold a single quart—and the valley was a hundred miles across!

He had saddlebags, of course. They were new and strong, of the heaviest canvas.

He took a pair of them and went to the nearest sound of running water. He drank and drank again of that delightfully bubbling spring; the mere sight of Alkali Flat had implanted in him an insatiable thirst. Then he filled one of the bags. The canvas was perfectly water-tight, but the seams let the water spurt out in streams.

He looked about him, not in despair, but with the sense of one condemned. If he could not enter the desert assured of a fair chance of getting through, why, he would enter it without that chance and trust to luck like a madman.

Then he saw the pine trees which were filling the mountain air with sweetness, and he remembered their resin.

Resin? It exuded from them in little fresh runs; it dripped from the wounded bark; it flavored the air with its clean scent. He began to collect it rapidly, with his knife, and as he got it, he commenced to smear the stuff over the seams of his saddlebags, which he turned inside out.

He had two pairs, and he resined all four in hardly more than an hour. That was why the stallion was wel' weighted down with a load of the purest spring water going down the slope toward Alkali Flat.

His master went ahead of him, jauntily, whistling a little; but the heat from the desert already was beginning to sting the eyes and make the lids of them tender.

35

In Alkali Flat, the earth was not a mother. It was a grave. Once there had been a river running through it; now there was only the hollow trough filled with the dead bones of the stream. Once there had been trees; now there were only the scarecrow trunks of a few ancient survivors.

As Sleeper passed down into the frightful glare of that wasted land, he saw the trail of Mahoney and Tim Riley lead up to the bank of the dead river and then pass down the length of it. He felt that he knew, at once, the nature of the windings which had been depicted on the chart and he could not help admiring the cleverness of Joe Mendoza, leaving his treasure here in the middle of a salt waste.

The temperature was above a hundred.

That is a phrase which people use casually, liberally, without understanding. Actually, every part of a degree above blood heat begins to draw the strength from the heart. A dry heat is then an advantage in a sense, because the quick evaporation of the perspiration cools the flesh a little.

But the heat in the great Alkali Flat was above a hundred and twenty. There were twenty-two degrees of fatal heat; and the dryness not merely turned sweat into mist at once, it laid hold on the flesh like a thousand leeches, sucking out the liquid from the body.

The feet of Sleeper began to burn in his boots. There seemed to be sand under his eyelids. The drying lips threatened to crack wide open. And thirst blew down his throat like a dusty wind at every breath he drew.

At the same time, the skin of his face commenced to pull and contract; and the dry skin of his body was rubbed and chafed by his clothes.

Careless, indomitable in all conditions, now held on his way with his ears laid flat against his skull.

When Sleeper looked up, he saw a wedge of three buzzards sliding out from the mountain height and hanging in the air. They might shun the air above the horrible flat, but not when foolish living creatures attempted to cross the floor of the oven.

What insane beings, even a Mahoney and a Riley, ventured on such a journey by the light of the day?

Sleeper looked from the dizzy sky back to the earth. It was like a kitchen yard, a yard on which thousands of gallons of soapy water, in the course of generations, have been flung upon a summer-baked soil, dishwater thrice a day. For a singular odor rose from the ground. And it was everywhere gray-white.

Along the banks of the river one could see where water had once flowed at varying levels. The banks had been eaten back by the now-dead stream. Here and there, at the edges of the levels, appeared the dry roots of long-vanished plants and trees, as fine as hair.

There was no steady breeze, but now and again a twist of the air sucked up dust in a small air pool that moved with swiftness for a short distance and then melted away. If one of those white phantoms swayed toward Sleeper, he swerved the horse to avoid it. Careless himself shrank from the contact, for the alkali dust burned the passages of nose and lungs and mouth like dry lye and the eyes were eaten by that unslaked lime.

Yet the other pair still advanced more deeply into that fire. An hour went by, and another, and another, and another. At a walk or a dogtrot, Careless stuck to his work. His coat was beginning to stare as his sweat dried and the salt of the perspiration stiffened the gloss of his hair. When Sleeper stroked the glorious neck of the horse, a thin dust followed his hand.

They had passed the danger point, long ago. That is to say, they had passed the point when a man could safely attempt to journey out of the alkali hell without water to carry. A fellow with a two-quart canteen, no matter how he nursed it, would probably be frantic for liquid before he reached the promise of the mountains which, already, were turning brown and blue in the distance.

And then the two figures far ahead, only discernible in the spyglass which Sleeper now and then used for spotting them, dipped away from the flat and disappeared. They had descended into the stream bed.

It might mean that they had spotted the pursuer and were going to stalk him in ambush. It might mean, also, that they had reached the proper bend of the dry draw and that they were about to search for the marked spot on the chart.

Sleeper, taking a chance on the second possibility, pushed Careless ahead rapidly until he was close to the point of the disappearance. Conscience, duty, a strange spirit seemed to ride in his shadow and drive him ahead, but his conscious mind rebelled against this torment. It told him to rush away toward one of those spots of cool, blue mirage which continually wavered into view on the face of the desert; it told him that all was useless, wealth, fame, honor no more real than the welter of the heat waves. But he kept on.

When he was reasonably close, he dipped Careless down into the channel of the vanished river, and watered him from the second saddlebag. The water was now almost the heat of blood and it had developed a foul taste from cooking inside the heavy canvas, but Careless supped up the water greedily until the bag was empty.

There remained to Sleeper one half of his original

205

supply; and yet one half of his labor had not been completed.

Under a steep of the bank where there was a fall of shadow, he placed the horse and made him lie down. But the shadow was not a great blessing. The dimness seemed to thicken the air; it was like breathing dust, and the sand, even under the shadow, was hot to the touch.

Here Careless was left, lifting his head and sending after his master a whinny of anxiety, no louder than a whisper. For the stallion knew as well as any man the reason those buzzards wheeled in the stillness of the hot air above.

Would the two men ahead take heed of the second group of the buzzards? Or would they fail to notice, earthbound as their eyes must be, that the vultures wheeled and sailed in two parts?

Sleeper went on swiftly, but with care. And he could wish, now, that he had not left Weldon with empty hands. He had his knife, to be sure, and if he came to close range, that heavy knife with its needlesharp point would be as deadly in his hands as any gun. It might well dispose of one of the pair; but the second one would certainly take revenge for his fall.

Very clearly, Sleeper knew what it meant if the couple were real companions of Joe Mendoza, that super-murderer. He would have none about him except experts in slaughter.

This knowledge made the step of Sleeper lighter than the step of a wildcat as he heard, directly around the next bend, the sound of blows sinking into the earth. From the sharp edge of the bank he saw, as he peered around it, both Mahoney and tall Tim Riley hard at work with a pick and a shovel which they had taken from their packs.

Their two horses, like the stallion, had been placed under the partial shadow of the western bank. One stood head down, like a dying thing; the other, with more of the invincible Western toughness supporting its knees and its spirit, wandered with slow steps down the draw, sniffing curiously at the strange dead roots that projected here and there from the bank.

The two workers, hard at it, had now opened a good-sized hole in the earth and they were driving it deeper and deeper when Mahoney uttered a wild cry and flung both arms above his head. Then, leaning, he tore at something buried in the earth. There was the brittle noise of the rending of a tough fabric; Mahoney jerked up holding what seemed a torn strip of tarpaulin in his hands, and leaned immediately to grasp it again. Riley helped him.

They were both yelling out senseless, meaningless words.

And now Sleeper saw a very strange thing to do, and did it. He slipped quietly out from his post of vantage and went up to the horse which was wandering with slow steps down the bank, the water sloshing with soft gurglings inside the burlap-wrapped huge canteen which hung from the saddle.

Sleeper took the horse calmly by the bridle and led it, step by step, around the bend. He had the horse almost out of view when Mahoney, leaping to his feet, apparently looked straight at the thief!

Instead of drawing a gun, Buzz Mahoney pulled off his hat and began to wave it and shout with delight. Tim Riley also commenced to prance around like a crazy man.

"The whole insides of the Levison Bank!" yelled Riley. "Kid, we got it! We're rich for life!"

They were blind with happiness. That was why Mahoney had failed to see the thief in his act of stealing, and now Sleeper was walking steadily down the draw with the horse behind him. He kept on until he reached the great stallion, which rose eagerly to meet him and touched noses with the other horse.

Then Sleeper mounted Careless and put two miles of steady cantering behind him. After that, he rode up the bank to the level of the ground above and waited.

He sat in the shade under the side of Careless and ventured to smoke a cigarette that filled his lungs with a milder fire than that of the alkali dust.

One horse, two men, and the long, burning stretch of the desert to cross before the blue peace of the mountains surrounded them. It seemed to Sleeper that there was nothing in the world so beautiful as mountains, these mountains to the north.

Time passed. He watered the two horses and himself drank, sparingly. There was still plenty of sun. It was high, high above the horizon, and those two fellows who had found the treasure of Joe Mendoza did not seem, as yet, to have discovered the loss of the second horse with more than half of their remaining water supply.

Well, the wind of joy would cool them for a spell, but afterward———

He thought, too, of the old, whiteheaded banker, Levison, still straight-backed, level-eyed, fearless of the hatred which men poured on him since the failure of his bank after the robbery.

What fools the officers of the law had been not to suspect that the job was that of Mendoza! Three men shot down wantonly. That was like Mendoza: and Riley and Mahoney were no doubt of the murderous crew that attended the chief on that day of the holdup.

It all made a simple picture, now. Escaping with their spoil, Mendoza had attended to the hiding of it. They would disappear from the face of the land for a time. Then, at an appointed date, they would regather.

But in the meantime, Mendoza had been captured on some other charge; he had been put into the prison and when he attempted to break out at the allotted moment, he had been shot. He had passed on his information, loyally, to his two men.

That was the story, and Sleeper knew it as well as though he had heard it from the lips of the pair.

And now, at last, the two came up over the edge of the draw and started toward the mountains, one of them in the saddle, the other riding behind.

Sleeper fell in behind them.

That terrible dryness of the air, that flaming of the sun no longer seemed hostile. It was performing his work.

At the end of a long, long hour, the mountains seemed even farther away than they had been at the beginning. And Sleeper saw the pair halt. They took off the big canteen from the side of their horse, drank, and then appeared to be measuring out some of the liquid for the horse.

From half a mile away, Sleeper distinctly could see the flash of the priceless water as it was poured. He could see the poor horse shake its head with eagerness for more. Then tall Tim Riley fastened the canteen back in its place beside the saddle.

This was the moment that Buzz Mahoney, snatching out a holstered rifle from the other side of the saddle, dropped to his knee and began to pour shot after shot at Sleeper.

But Sleeper, at a thousand yards, laughed, and the laughter was a dry whisper in his throat.

He took off his hat and waved it, as though in encouragement. And the two remounted, and went on.

36

For nearly another hour, Sleeper traveled in the wake of the pair; and still they seemed to be laboring in vain, never bringing the mountains closer.

Then trouble struck suddenly. They had dismounted to take water and give it to the horse again when Sleeper saw by their gestures that they were in a heated argument. Two guns flashed like two dancing bits of blue flame. Then he saw Mahoney fall on his face; afterward the swift rattle of the reports struck his ear.

Tim Riley mounted and continued on his way, looking back toward the spot where his victim lay.

Sleeper, for some reason, looked suddenly up toward the buzzards which wheeled softly in the sky above him. They would be fed, now.

But the figure of Mahoney now lifted from the ground. He ran a few steps in pursuit of Riley, and the small sound of his distant wailing came into the ears of Sleeper.

To get mercy from Riley was an impossibility which not even the bewildered brain of a wounded man could entertain long. Sleeper, with a queer sickness of the heart, saw Mahoney tear the shirt from his back and fall to digging in the sand.

Already the shock and the pain of bullet wounds, the swift loss of blood, and the burning caustic of the heat of Alkali Flat had reduced him to the madness of famine.

Sleeper came up rapidly, calling out; he was almost at the point where Mahoney groveled in the sand on his knees, scooping at the earth with his hands, before the wounded man looked up. He saw Sleeper with the bewilderment with which he might have stared at a heavenly angel. Then he came with a scream of hope distending his mouth and eyes, his arms thrown out.

Blood ran down his body, which was swollen with strength rather than with fat. But he disregarded his wounds until he had drunk deeply. Then, recovering his wits a little, he looked rather vaguely up to Sleeper.

"You're still back on the trail, eh?" said Mahoney. "Leave me ride that other horse, will you?"

"You can ride it if you want," agreed Sleeper.

There might have been twenty murders on the hands of this fellow, but still Sleeper pitied him.

Mahoney grasped the pommel of the saddle on the led horse, but suddenly weakness overcame him. He looked down with a singular wonder at the blood which rolled down his body. Those wounds were beyond curing, as Sleeper had seen at a glance. Mahoney realized it now, also, and the realization struck him down to his knees. He slumped to the side, his mouth open as he dragged at the hot, dusty air.

Sleeper, dismounting, knelt by him.

Mahoney cursed him. "Leave me be. I'm cooked," he said. "Go get Riley. Riley—he murdered me. I'm the eleventh man on his list. Him and Mendoza was like a coupla brothers. If I could live to see Riley crawl———— But I sure snagged him with my second shot. He's hur⁺ And them that are hurt in Alkali Flat————"

He dropped flat on his back, and Sleeper thought tha he was gone. But after a moment he spoke again, saying "He thinks he'll get loose—but in Alkali Flat—death—death—will get through a scratch on the skin. Riley—Riley————"

A little shudder went through him, as though he had been touched by cold.

And Sleeper turned to remount, for he knew that Mahoney was dead.

Had Buzz really struck Tim Riley with one of his bullets? It seemed very likely, considering that they had exchanged shots almost hand to hand. And yet Tim Riley was voyaging steadily on across the Flat.

The mountains were closer, now. But in Alkali Flat the heat increased. The life was gone from the air. As the sun slanted from a deeper position in the west, a sort of mist seemed to cover the desert. That was the dust, made visible in the slanting sun rays, and this film of dust was what made breathing so difficult, perhaps.

Mahoney was dead. A division of the buzzards had dropped toward the ground; but still others trailed after Tim Riley.

Had they scented the death which might even now be working in the body of Riley?

As Mahoney had well said, through the smallest scratch death could enter the bodies of men in Alkali Flat. Where the struggle for mere existence was so hard, the slightest wound, the slightest extra drain on the strength might prove fatal.

Yet Tim Riley, so far as Sleeper could see, even through the glass, rode erect and steady.

Sleeper closed his thousand yards of safety to a quarter of a mile, to study the gunman. But he had a strong feeling that he was about to lose his long battle. For now the mountains rose like a wall against the sky; the heat of the sun was diminishing; twilight would unroll like a blessing across Alkali Flat before long, and Tim Riley would be among the slopes of the foothills, hunting for the sound of running water in the night, climbing steadily toward a purer, cooler air.

Where the flat ended, Sleeper saw the white streak of it just ahead, like a watermark drawn across the hills; and Tim Riley was approaching that mark when, all at once, Sleeper saw that the horse was plodding on with downward head, as before, but with an empty saddle.

But no, it was not empty. The rider had slumped well

forward and lay out on the neck of the horse.

It might be a bit of playing possum, Sleeper thought. For Riley must have realized that his pursuer was not armed, and now this might be a device to draw the other into easy range.

So Sleeper pressed forward only slowly until he noticed that the buzzards were swaying lower and lower through the air above the head of the fugitive.

As though they conveyed a direct message to him, Sleeper lost all fear at once and closed in abruptly.

As he came, he saw the rider slipping slowly, inch by inch, toward the side.

When Sleeper came up, he waited until he actually had a hand on the shoulder of Tim Riley before he called out. But Tim Riley continued to lie prone, as though resting from a great fatigue.

He was resting indeed, for he was dead.

When Sleeper stopped the horses at the base of the first foothill, he found that Tim Riley had been shot deeply through the body, a wound which might not have been fatal under ordinary circumstances, but which surely meant death in Alkali Flat.

And Riley had known that. He had lashed himself in his saddle. With his hands on the pommel, he had ridden erect, keeping his face toward safety and the mountains.

The mere instinct to keep on fighting had driven him on. A queer admiration crept through the heart of Sleeper as he looked at the lean, hard face of Riley, still set and grim and purposeful in death.

In the saddlebag strapped behind the saddle was what Sleeper had struggled and striven so hard to reach.

He knew that but left the thing untouched, while he urged the tired horse up the hill. He walked beside the horse that carried the dead man, to make sure that the body did not slip to the ground. A last, grim hour they struggled up that slope until Sleeper heard the sound

213

of running water; and a moment later the horses were standing bellydeep in a pool of blue, while Sleeper drank and drank again from the rivulet that fed the little lake.

By the side of that lake he buried Tim Riley by the simple device of laying the body under a boulder above which a little slide of rocks was hanging. A few stones moved, and that slide was launched. Fifty tons of débris rushed down over the spot where Riley lay; and his funeral oration was the flying echoes which talked and sang busily together for a few seconds all along the canyon.

By the little pool, when it was holding the stars and the thin yellow flickering of the camp fire, Sleeper ate hard tack, drank coffee, and examined the contents of the big saddlebag.

It was, in fact, the savings of an entire life of crime. He counted, bill by bill, three hundred and fifteen thousand dollars of hard cash. And, in addition, there were a number of jewels, choice stones which had been broken out of their settings.

The blood began to beat fast in the temples of Sleeper.

37

Levison, president and chief shareholder in the Levison Bank of Tucker Flat, still went down to his office, every day. He carried himself exactly as he had done when the lifting of his finger was enough to control the wild men and the strong men of Tucker Flat.

He had a short, black mustache, his eyebrows and eyes were black, but his hair was a thin cloud of white. He was a narrow, tall, straight man who had looked the world in the face for so many years that disaster could not teach him to bow his head. When he walked down the street, now, people scowled at him; they cursed him in audible undertones; but he walked neither more quickly nor more slowly. His wife knew that Levison was dying of a broken heart, but he was dying on his feet.

Every day he went down to the bank, unlocked the front door, walked past the grille work of gilded steel, past the empty cages of the cashier and clerk, and into his own office, where he unlocked his desk and waited.

Sometimes he was there all day, and nothing happened; but often some one entered to talk over the recent robbery and to curse Levison for not guarding the treasures of others more securely.

Levison used to answer: "If there is any fault, it is mine. You have a right to denounce me. No man should dare to fail in this world of ours!"

And he kept his chin high, while grief like an inward wolf devoured his heart.

On this day, his walk down the street had been particularly a trial. For the unemployed from the closed mines were thick in the street and they had learned to attribute their lack of a job to the failure of the bank which had shut up the mines. So they thronged thickly about Levison, shook their fists in his face, cursed him and all his ancestors. He went through them like a sleepwalker and never answered a word. Perhaps he hoped that one of the drunkards would strike him down and that the rest would pluck the life out of his body; it was not rooted very deep in his flesh, these days.

So, when he came to his office, he sat with his head bowed a little and his hands folded together on the edge of his desk. He wanted to die, quickly; but there was that hollow-cheeked woman who waited for him in the house on the hill from which the servants had been discharged. Wherever he went, even into death, she would follow him not more than a step behind.

He heard the front door of the bank open in the middle of the morning. A step sounded in the emptiness of the big outer room, and then a hand tapped at his door.

"Come in!" called Levison.

The door was pushed open by a slender young fellow with black hair and blue eyes. He was very brown of skin, erect of carriage; and his clothes were mere ragged patches.

Over his shoulder he carried a saddlebag.

"Were you a depositor in my bank?" asked Levison, opening the usual formula.

"I never was, but I intend to be," said the stranger.

Levison frowned. "The bank has failed," he said gravely.

"Then we'd better bring it back to life again," said the other.

"Who are you?" snapped Levison.

"Name of Sleeper. And here's the stuff that Joe Mendoza and Tim Riley and Buzz Mahoney stole from your vault. All of that and a little more. How much did you lose?"

Levison rose slowly from his chair. He stared into the blue eyes of this young man, and it seemed to him that they were the blue of flame before it turns yellow.

"Two hundred and fifty-two thousand, five hundred and fourteen dollars," he said. That number was written somewhere across his soul as across a parchment.

"Count it out of this lot, then," said Sleeper. "There's plenty more. And then tell me where the rest of the cash ought to go—or have I claim to it? It's the life savings of Mr. Murderer Mendoza!"

At the little shack outside the town of Tucker Flat, Pop Lowry strode back and forth and up and down.

216

Three men waited near the small camp fire, never speaking, looking curiously across at Lowry now and then.

"I been double-crossed," said Pop Lowry. "I ought to send you out on his trail right now. But I'm gonna wait to see has he got the nerve to come here and face me! I'm gonna wait another half hour."

"Hark at them sing!" said one of the men, lifting his head.

For from the town of Tucker Flat there poured distant rumblings and even thin, high-pitched, half-hysterical laughter.

For the bank of Levison had reopened, and the mines that had recovered their deposits were reopening, also. That was reason enough to make the men of Tucker Flat rejoice.

Here there was a slight noise of rustling leaves among the shrubbery, and then into the dimness of the firelight rode a man on a great golden stallion.

"Sleeper!" exclaimed Pop Lowry.

"Get the three of them out of the way," said Sleeper, halting Careless.

"Back up, boys," said the peddler. "Wait somewheres—somewheres that I can whistle to you."

The three rose, stared an instant at Sleeper like dogs marking a quarry, and then stalked away.

Sleeper went to the fire, rinsed a tin cup, and filled it with coffee. He made and lighted a cigarette to accompany the coffee, and blew the smoke into the air after a deep inhalation.

"Well?" said Lowry, growling. "You done yourself fine, I hear?"

"Who told you I did?" asked Sleeper.

"Nobody else would 'a' got the money back. Nobody else would 'a' got it back for Levison and then told him to swear not to use the name. *You* got the money Mendoza stole!"

"Levison has his quarter of a million," said Sleeper.

"And there was something left over. You get half."

He took out a sheaf of bills tied about by a piece of string and threw it like a stick of wood to the peddler.

"There's a shade over sixty thousand in that," said Sleeper. "Count out your half. Besides, there's this stuff. Levison says that I have a right to it. So you take half of this, too—seeing that I'm your hired man!"

He threw a little chamois sack into the hands of Lowry, who lifted his head once, and thrust out his long jaw before he began to reckon the treasure.

After that, he was employed for a long time. At last he looked up and said hoarsely: "Where's Mahoney?"

"In Alkali Flat," said Sleeper.

"Dead?"

"Yes."

"Where's Tim Riley?"

"In the hills near Alkali Flat."

"Dead?"

"Yes."

"You let 'em find the stuff, and then you took it away from 'em?"

"Yes."

"And you didn't use a gun?"

"No."

"What *did* you use?"

"The sun and the buzzards," said Sleeper.

Lowry rubbed a hand back across the bald spot of his head.

"You had the brains to do that—and you was still fool enough to turn back a quarter of a million to that Levison?"

Sleeper sipped black coffee.

"You don't even get any glory out of it!" shouted Lowry. "You won't let Levison tell who done the job for him. There ain't a soul in the world but me that knows what you done!"

"Pop," said Sleeper, "glory is a dangerous thing for a fellow like me."

The peddler stared at him.

"A hundred and twenty-five thousand to you—the same to me—and you throwed it away! You ain't human! You're a fool!"

Sleeper sipped more coffee and drew on his cigarette.

"Tell me," growled Pop Lowry. "What you expect to get out of life? If you don't want money, what *do* you want?"

"Fun," said Sleeper thoughtfully.

"This here hell trail, this here work you done in Alkali Flat that even the birds—save the buzzards—won't fly over—was that fun? Where was the fun in that?"

"The look in the eyes of Levison," said Sleeper thoughtfully. "That was the fun for me, Pop."